CASTOFFS OF THE GODS

SONJA DEWING

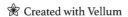

GET THE PREQUEL

Get the page turning adventure prequels to the Idol Maker series for free. Sign up for my email list at www.sonjadewing.com/contact

ACKNOWLEDGEMENTS

This book should have taken a year, but it took two years. All because of that terrible pandemic that sucked away my writing muse.

Thank you to my friends who got me out of my funk; Ben, Rebecca, and Sam. To my wonderfully sweet puppy Bo, who made me laugh every day, and still does.

To my fantastic writing group that helped me keep this book on track.

And, to my awesome early readers who caught my goof ups (like saying Leslie had beagles instead of basset hounds). I was probably thinking of my own beagle we had when I was a kid.

1

PROLOGUE

Benedict quietly cursed the heat of the jungle as he wiped his brow of sweat. He walked across the campsite, taking note that one of his men had recently put up a pole in the middle of camp with a talisman carved into it. It was probably meant to protect from the evil that permeated the Amazon jungle. It didn't appear to be aiding them.

He reached into his pup tent and pulled out a new journal from his backpack. His other journals were already full of observations, ideas, notes, and locations. Most of them he had already sent back home with hired runners. No doubt his completed journals were spread out all over the hemisphere on their slow journey to his wife in England.

He hated being away from his wife and the rest of his children, but it couldn't be helped. It was his theory of a hidden civilization that had brought him, his eldest son, and this group of hired men into the heart of the Amazon jungle. He wanted to find proof of a large city before anyone else. Most people thought the idea was mad. How could a civilization have existed in such an inhospitable place? But he knew it was out here.

On his first trip to the Amazon to collect seeds and rubber tree plantings for the British Government he and his team had happened upon a hand carved stone, ten-feet tall, fallen on its side. He kept the imprints of that stone with him at all times. It was evidence that there had been more than unsophisticated natives roaming the jungle. At least, finding the two pyramids had been further proof, proof that couldn't be easily dismissed. His men were excavating the largest and with whatever they would find, maybe now the Royal Geographic Society would stop thumbing their noses at him.

He opened the new journal to the first page. No matter how securely he wrapped them in wax paper to protect them from the humidity, they always felt soggy.

Benedict Cecil Spafford – August 1, 1911

The discovery of the rubber tree has filled the Amazon with a smattering of dirty shantytowns brimming with men looking for money and willing to tame the wilderness. But the wilderness is far from tame.

From Nauta we look toward millions of miles of tangled jungle, hiding wild boar and jaguar, insects that bury themselves in your skin, and tribes that would cook you for dinner. The jungle is itself my nemesis, a far greater enemy than the men I compete against.

I know that somewhere, out here, lies the city that matches the greatness of the pyramids. Percy Fawcett believes he will find it first. We will see who's the better man. Besides, he isn't after truth; he's just after treasure and any prestige he can garner for his society.

Benedict paused in his writing. Should he say what he thought of Percy? If these pages were read in the future, he didn't want anyone to think less of him for sharing the truth about another man.

He stared up at his find. His men were clearing debris and

trees from one of the towering Inca pyramids. Percy had yet to find anything like this, although the American, Hiram Bingham, had just found the ruins of a mountain-top city called Machu Picchu high above the Amazon basin.

Benedict crossed out the mention of Percy. He didn't need to disparage anyone. And besides, it was just his opinion.

Of course, Percy Fawcett might just beat me to it. I have heard he is searching in the far reaches on the other side of the Amazon basin, many miles from here. I wish him luck, but I'm sure he must deal with the same trials as any contingent of men in this jungle.

So far I have lost five men. Usually, I could say how it happened. In the past, men have died from a venomous bite or a fever. However, my men are now disappearing almost one a day without explanation or anyone seeing what happened. At first, the porters I hired from Nauta told my men they were worried about an angry god roaming the jungle, then the porters began vanishing.

Now, even some of my men hired in England are disappearing. Yesterday, there was an unnatural silence of the jungle followed by a blood-curdling scream. I sent Joshua and Leo to investigate. Neither returned. I pray to God that they simply couldn't take this adventure anymore and have headed back home.

The rest of the men are wary and no one is going anywhere unless there is a band of others with them.

Someone asked me this morning if I believed in the old gods. "No," I told him, "Gods are a way for the natives to explain nature. If there is something dangerous here, it's a wild cat, or some other predator. Something we can fight and overcome as men." Every word I say must be encouraging because I need every man I have to help on this excavation.

"Father?!"

Benedict scribbled his last thoughts.

If anyone else disappears, we'll have to head back home to start again. Most importantly, I don't want anything to happen to my son.

He is too young for his life to end in this jungle and I, for one, would be cursed if he didn't make it out.

"Yes, William?" Benedict wrapped the journal in the wax paper and tucked it into his pocket.

"The men have cleared a path through the entrance to the inside of the pyramid. I think it's time for us to go explore."

Benedict was proud of his son's initiative and excitement. At only eighteen he had far proven his worth on this trip.

Benedict nodded. "That's a capital plan. Let's take five of the men with us." He tucked the notebook, pen, and ink in his pocket.

"Yes, Father."

William took off at a run in the direction of the pyramid. Benedict smiled at the youthful energy his son had in this heat-oppressive place. He yelled out to William. "Start off without me, I need to grab my kit."

Benedict was reaching for his bag when he saw the silhouette of a man standing at the edge of the clearing. The stranger was dark-skinned, wore a tall blue and gold headdress, and a white dress with a red belt. If the man had weapons they were not visible.

Even though he had been through dozens of first contacts, Benedict felt trepidation at the sight of the tribe member. The stranger wasn't from any tribe that he knew of. The clothing was more regal, cleaner, than of any tribe he had met so far. William had already disappeared and Benedict was too far away from any of his men to get their attention. It would also be a mistake to put his back to a native to go find help. Some locals considered turning away to be rude and he couldn't risk angering him. The only answer was to approach the man and use his best first contact skills.

Benedict walked up the hill. At any moment he expected

this man's followers to appear around him, as natives rarely traveled alone.

The man stoically watched him, his arms crossed, as Benedict approached. He had deep lines on his face and a touch of grey hair, but it was impossible to tell age in the jungle. The stress from living in this environment could age one quickly.

"Who are you?" The native asked the question in English, although heavily accented with the local tongue.

Benedict's jaw dropped. He had never heard a native use English. "I'm Benedict Cecil Spafford. I'm an explorer."

"Tell me why you explore my people's lands."

The man was not more than five-feet tall, but Benedict could feel the power hovering as if the man were a giant. The native seemed relaxed and exuded confidence. Benedict felt his brow wrinkle. He must have an army of his people waiting to pounce.

Benedict glanced back but no one from his camp was in sight. He chose his words with great care.

"We English like to learn about other civilizations and we'd love to learn about your people. We come with gentle intentions. I would like to meet your people." Benedict glanced around at the surrounding jungle.

"I will show you the place of my people." The man pointed at the pyramid. "They once worshipped here. But I will warn you, many men before you have been here. Too late I learned not to trust outsiders. While you are here, you will be judged."

"Judged?"

The native turned and walked away. Would this man really show him his people? Would he lead him to the city that went with the ruined pyramids? The city he had been searching for.

He'd worry about judging later. He glanced back again, but still none of his men were in sight. Blast! He should have asked his son to wait. But he may never have this opportunity again.

He pulled the compass out of his vest and followed the man into the dark jungle.

They walked for what seemed hours, but the jungle could make minutes feel like days. With every step Benedict was fighting with the humidity in order to breathe, as well as all the vines and limbs that seemed intent on impeding his progress.

The path they followed was thin and unkept. That didn't make a lot of sense if this man's tribe still used the city, but maybe they didn't go to the pyramid anymore. This man, probably a chieftain by the looks of his bright headdress, was perhaps the only one who still worshipped there.

Benedict stumbled over a stone. The chieftain caught his arm to keep him from falling. Their eyes met and Benedict saw both concern and anger in the man's eyes.

"How much farther?" Benedict asked.

"We are here." The chieftain said.

Benedict looked around. It took a moment for the outline of chest-high, eroded stonewalls to be visible in the dark jungle.

The chieftain's shoulders sagged. "This is all that is left.."

Benedict looked out over the few crumbled buildings that he could see. "How many people lived here?"

No answer came. Benedict turned three hundred and sixty degrees but there was no chieftain. It wasn't unusual for the locals to disappear by blending in with the surrounding jungle, but it still got on his nerves.

The chieftain was likely watching from a distance, waiting for him to leave. But now Benedict's curiosity was piqued. Sure these were just a few homes, but certainly, this had to extend for miles in order to house the number of people who had lived to serve and worship at the pyramids.

He looked at his compass and decided to keep heading in the same direction. He skirted the small stone ruins and followed a series of broken walls. He mentally planned how his men would excavate a few of the buildings to see if they could find anything to explain the history here. More than likely, tribes who came through here had taken stones from the old buildings to use them in their own building material. That would explain the degradation of these buildings in relation to the pyramid. The pyramid stones were too big to be picked up and carried by just a few tribes members.

How long had this place been inhabited? Where had the others gone who had lived here?

He stumbled again, falling onto his knees. When he stood back up the valley ahead of him had transformed. Suddenly, the broken buildings were whole again. There were multi-story grey stone buildings. Hundreds of residents were walking in the stone streets.

"By God, this is amazing." He reached for the closest wall to steady himself, half expecting his hand to move through this ghostly vision. But it felt solid and warm. He ran his hand over the grey stone, appreciating the chiseled, clean lines and the tight fit of the stones.

The street curved downward toward a town square, then curved back up on the other side. In the square there was a fountain with the face of a jaguar. Water poured from its mouth into a bowl and all of it made of gold. The water looked like glimmering silver. Behind that, a two-story square building shined with gold as well.

Benedict walked up to the fountain. None of the natives paid him any mind.

Of course, this was just a dream. A civilization like this couldn't exist in his day and not be known. To test his theory he reached a hand out to a native walking nearby, dressed much the same as the chieftain, but without the headdress. She turned away from his hand as if she could see him, but didn't look his way. He reached out to a man passing by and once again, the native turned away as if seeing his hand, but didn't acknowledge his presence.

His wife would tell him he was a crackpot when she heard about this.

The city and its structure were more sophisticated than he had imagined. The narrow streets were made of small chiseled grey stone, flat and even. The buildings were solid structures and in different sizes and configurations. He assumed some were for storage, others for homes, and others possibly administrative in nature.

He turned his attention back to the fountain and examined the gold. It was warm where the sun touched it and cold where the water pooled. Benedict splashed some water on himself and smiled at its cool touch. He took his handkerchief from his pocket and soaked it in the water, washing his face. The respite from the heat was refreshing. This was exactly what made a civilization grow, the ability to control access to water. But how could such a civilization control water?

The thin layers of gold were affixed over a harder surface, probably of stone. What he really wanted to see was how the fountain functioned.

He got down on his knees and looked at the seams of the fountain. He pulled out his knife and dug at the seam to see what was inside. He pealed back some of the gold.

Benedict heard a sound like thunder. He looked up. The sound had come from the chieftain who was floating in mid-air.

Benedict stepped back, his heart beating fast. What magic did this chieftain have?

"It is invaders like you that did this to my people."

The scene changed. Men in armor were forcing the residents out of their homes and onto their knees in the square.

One conquistador was attempting to pry the gold off of the fountain, damaging the stone underneath in his rush.

Benedict realized that the chieftain was comparing him to the people who had raped these lands long before he had arrived. "No. No, that's not it. I only wanted—"

"That's not why you have been judged," the chieftain's voice boomed. A crate flew through the air and landed at Benedict's feet with a thump. It was a crate of canned fruit Benedict had purchased from the Pihuaya Rubber Tree Company, marked with their symbol of a silver cup tipping over with black latex flowing from the inside. "I know what you've done!"

The scene changed. Benedict was now standing in the middle of what was certainly a rubber tree town. But this town was different. A group of natives stumbled and held each other up as a man herded them with a whip. These natives were chained, obviously force labor for extracting rubber tree sap. Benedict had heard of this happening but had never seen it in person. It was deplorable. The town was populated with tents and every one had the silver cup symbol imprinted on them.

Benedict realized that these people were of the chieftain's tribe, and that he was boom judged for what was happening to them. "It wasn't me!" he screamed, knowing that these people wouldn't react to him. They were only a reflection, an extension of the chieftain's magic. But there was no response from the chieftain either. "I apologize that this has happened! I don't work with that company. I don't represent them and their behavior!"

The ground under him opened and he fell backward. He screamed as a spike burst up through his thigh. Benedict fell hard onto the ground; he could hardly breathe through the pain.

"No," he whispered weakly. He could feel his strength slipping away as his blood pooled and soaked the back of his clothes. The spike must have punctured an artery. He'd never be able to get himself off of the six-foot tall stake. He touched the spike gently with his shaking hands, hoping it wasn't real, but it was solid.

He knew he would never see his son again. He could feel the pain with every short breath.

Knowing his life would soon be over, he drew out the notebook and writing instrument from his pocket. He shakily wrote down the secret that must be shared before he lost consciousness.

He pulled out the stone imprints and protective wax paper and wrapped them all carefully. He laid them on his chest and allowed himself to rest his head back.

Now, he noticed the other bodies lying in the pit. One of his men's empty eyes looked through him. He could see a small pith helmet lying on the ground. Close to it was a smooth young hand, the rest of the body hidden behind another. "William," he could only whisper. Benedict felt the tears coming and then he couldn't stop. He cried for his men and he cried for his son who would never see England again. His chest heaved from crying and pain shot through his body.

Then the chieftain stood next to him. He looked down at Benedict. "Be at peace."

Benedict felt the pain evaporate into darkness.

2

JOHN'S DISAPPEARANCE

John pushed aside the vines and peered into the valley that spread out below.

"Damn it."

It wasn't the right area. There were no remnants of buildings that he could see. Just flat ground. Behind him lay a sharp hill, too steep for any buildings to have been built on. He glanced at the GPS. He was exactly where he had planned to be, but nothing was here.

The sun was high, and he took out a handkerchief to wipe the sweat from his forehead.

The vines fell back into place as he turned to face the choked jungle. He had been so sure he would find it here. He'd have to head back and regroup to figure out where to try next. But he didn't want to head back. It would take several days to get to his ship and then another two days to reach civilization. He could make his way to the pyramids— they weren't far, maybe a couple of miles. So about five hours of cutting through vines to get there. But he knew he could find some shelter and he could fish in the river before he headed back.

He didn't like either idea. He kicked at a tree, then kicked at it again. This time he missed and knocked into a pile of limbs and vines. His foot hit something solid.

He bent down to look. Brushing back the vines, a three-foot face of a snake looked up at him. Very similar to the snake carving that was near the pyramids. A stone carving that looked incredibly real. He touched it just to be sure. The snake was cold stone.

He looked up at the jungle canopy. Could this be part of the city? Finding the carved stone meant he had to be close. Maybe he expected too much. He had imagined the buildings would still be viewable. Maybe the stone walls were so degraded that they were hidden beneath the walls of vines.

He cleared more of the area around the snake and then swung his machete to break more of the vines so he could see under the brush. Under the snake was a pile of small stones. Like the kind they would have used for homes in the ancient world, in Viracocha's day.

John looked closely at the snakehead. It was probably an icon of Viracocha. He reflected on the tragedy that had befallen these ancient people and wondered if Viracocha was truly gone. Just last year, John had been in the jungle and had seen the wrath of the Inca god and had almost died under the creator god's angry gaze.

He was glad it wasn't a real snake. Leslie would be mad as hell if he disappeared into a giant snake's belly. His conversation with Leslie before heading into the jungle had given him something to look forward to after this trip.

Two weeks had gone by since he had called her to see if he could talk her into going with him into the jungle.

Leslie had responded adamantly, "No way! I've had my fill of jungle. I'm planning a trip to Greenland where there are no gods, no snakes, no piranhas, and no traps."

"How do you know there are no gods there? Like me, you probably didn't believe in any of the old gods until we had one join us on the trip into the Amazon. And besides, what if Viracocha decides to take a vacation in Greenland?"

"No. I'm pretty sure he's gone." She hadn't expanded on why.

"I'm surprised. You're as interested in Benedict's journals as I am. That latest one I sent you, did you read it? He talks about finding a stone monolith during his work as a map maker. Something no one has ever seen since. Aren't you at least curious about what lies here in the Amazon?"

"Of course, I am. But I also know my limits. That place taxes everything you have. Once was plenty for me. Now, who are you taking with you?"

"I'm not sure. Maybe I'll go alone."

"Well, that's a terrible idea." She had left the silence in the air while John considered.

He finally filled the void. "Look, there are few people I trust. Jessup is gone. One of my best guides, Sun, is gone. Cesario is gone. That was a rough ride. Besides, I know the terrain, and I'll have my satellite phone."

"What about Miguel?"

"I've heard he's in Nauta working on a project of his own. I decided not to bother him, let him have some time to heal over losing his brother."

"At least promise me you'll send word via radio or satellite every day. And, if you're not back to Nauta by a certain day, I'll come find you." He could hear the concern in her voice.

"Does that mean you're going to worry about me?" he chided innocently.

She answered in a serious tone, "Of course I'm going to worry about you running off into the Amazon. Benedict Cecil Spafford was a trained explorer with a great deal of money and support behind his travels. He never came out of the jungle. What makes you think you will?"

"I know. This will be dangerous. I just feel I'm so close to finding Spafford. We never found anything of substance at the pyramids, so I'm thinking I might have luck looking for the lost city. One of his last journals mentioned having clues to the whereabouts of the city that used the pyramids as a worship center. It's got to be somewhere near the pyramids."

"Please be careful. When you get back, I want to meet up and hear all about it." Leslie said.

"Is that a promise? Because if so, let's meet somewhere nice, like Hawaii. I'll get us our own little bungalow." John held his breath, realizing he was putting it all out there with that statement. It felt like it took her forever to answer.

"Whoa, John. That sounds amazing! I'd love to join you. Let's do it."

John let out a sigh of relief. "Good. Now I have a real reason to come back."

She laughed, and he rung off with excitement for the future.

Now he just wanted to find this damn city. He slapped the figure of the snakehead and wondered if it had rolled down the hill that faced him. It was steep. He grasped trees to help him walk up the hill. It was slow going until he reached the top, then took a moment to wipe the sweat from his forehead again and reposition his hat.

He made his way through the jungle looking for more signs of old city structures. A glint of something on the ground sparkling in a ray of sunlight drew his attention. Two steps forward, and the ground under him gave way. He fell, barely managing to grasp the edge of the pit with his right hand.

He hung by three fingers. He reached up with his other

hand, but it was too late. He fell again, the ground coming up fast, the darkness in the pit an eternity.

3

BAD NEWS

Leslie was feeding her basset hounds, Donald and Daisy, both stepping on each other in their excitement for dinner, when her phone rang. The number identified as being from Peru, and it wasn't a number she had seen before. She put the dog bowls down on the floor and took a deep breath as she put the phone to her ear.

"Hello," she said.

"Leslie?" the familiar sound of a Spanish accented male voice asked.

"Miguel! It's good to hear from you. Thank you for calling me."

"Hello. It's good to hear your voice. I got your message through the hotel. I followed up on your request to check on John. No one's heard from him for the last three days."

"Damn it." Leslie sat on the floor next to the dogs. Her concern for John felt like a knot in her stomach— and knowing that she'd have to trek into the jungle again had deflated her normal high energy. Daisy left her bowl of food, crawling into

Leslie's lap. "I hope he's okay. And when I find him, he's going to be in big trouble."

"Does that mean you're coming to Peru to find him?"

"Yes, and Miguel, I could use your help."

"You've got it."

"Great! I have a list of equipment I'll need and I'll have some other details. Where can I send that?" She jotted down his contact information and signed off, glad of hearing Miguel's voice. Knowing that he was willing to help was good news; Miguel would be invaluable with his expertise from his years of exploring the Amazon.

She had been surprised he was still in Nauta. After his brother's death at the hands of an Inca god, she had thought he'd take a break from that environment and come back to the states where he and his brother had grown up. However, she figured she'd have plenty of time to find out why he was still there when she arrived in Peru. It would take a week or more to reach John's last known location. He could only hope he was still alive.

She hugged Daisy, scooted the dog off her lap and got up. Now she could feel her nervous energy building. She immediately put her plan into play.

Her first call was to her friend, AJ Bluehorse, who was expecting a call if something went wrong with John's solo expedition. As soon as AJ answered Leslie said, "John's disappeared. He's been out of contact for five days. We had an agreement that he'd send word every day. So he's overdue."

Leslie held her breath. Out of everyone she wanted with her on this rescue mission, she could trust AJ the most— and AJ knew what she would be getting into.

"I'll be there. And I promise my boots will be broken in this time."

Leslie let out her breath. "They better be!" she joked,

remembering the trouble AJ had when she had brought new boots to the Amazon the last time. "I'll send you all the information. I'm treating this like any other excursion, so I'll have all the equipment we need when you get there."

"Let me know if you need any funds," AJ said.

"Will do."

Leslie called the airport and made arrangements. Then while she patted Donald's soft ears, she called a friend to dog sit while she was gone.

Adrenaline pumped through her now. Her flight wouldn't leave until tomorrow morning and even then, it would be a long day of travel before she could do anything of use.

She got out her backpack and suitcase and began a frenzied rush of putting everything she'd need to take in a pile. With superhuman speed she had everything packed and was as ready as she could be, but the stress was still making her heart pound.

She put on her sneakers, braided her long hair and pinned it up, and headed out the door. A run would help calm her nerves.

As she started her run, she wondered about John, and what he might be going through in the jungle. If she found him, if he was still alive, she'd talk him into never going back. His urge to find clues about his great uncle, Benedict Cecil Spafford, in the jungle wasn't worth the risk of dying from any of the million things one could die from in the Amazon.

She had certainly never wanted to go back. At least she now had plenty of experience in setting out on adventures and long treks. So she figured this trip should go better than the last time she was stranded in the Amazon without the right equipment. Hopefully.

4

NOTHING IS SMOOTH

Leslie finished her fourth walk around the Lima, Peru airport, keeping an eye on her gate. Luckily, the line to board was getting shorter.

She tossed her empty coffee cup into the trash, joined the boarding line, and scanned her ticket for the gate worker. As she entered the plane, she recognized a man in a green t-shirt with "Arizona Archeology Expo" across the back— he had been on her fight from LAX. He was helping an older gentleman put his heavy carryon into the overhead bin.

By the time she reached the row he was sitting in she was disappointed to see that there wasn't an open seat next to him. She assumed from his dark complexion and features that he was Peruvian and that he might have some interesting stories to tell.

While she stood in the aisle waiting for those in front of her to move she sent a quick text message to AJ to let her know she was taking off soon.

From her window seat, she watched Lima disappear under

her and the ocean glow in the sunshine. Little dots of surfers were all along the ocean's edge and a fog was rolling into the city.

She stared into the cloud cover, letting herself relax for just a moment. This one-hour flight would go by quickly, and as soon as the flight touched down she had work to do. The sunlight on the clouds became blinding so she pulled down the shade.

Normally, she would have had all the equipment sent to her so she could inspect it, then ship it to the destination; but time was too limited, so she had ordered everything to arrive at the airport in Puerto Maldonaldo. As soon as she arrived, she would review the equipment and see that it was loaded onto the next flight safely.

She was not leaving anything to chance.

Like the amulet hanging from her necklace. It had taken long nights pouring over old dusty books in some of the oldest bookstores she could find to discover any inkling of how to protect herself from magic. She then had to find a willing artist to make it to her specifications. She didn't know if the carnelian stone and copper pendant would actually protect her from future run-ins with gods— if there were any left roaming the earth, like Viracocha. But she wasn't going back out without at least trying to protect herself.

When Viracocha had grown into a giant and sent a man to his death, she had felt helpless and vulnerable.

As she felt the plane begin to descend, she peeked under the shade on her window. The small airport of Puerto Maldanaldo had to be close. Off in the distance she could see the edge of the Amazon basin. Tall dark trees packed closely together. Beyond that initial line of trees, as far as the eye could see, was nothing but dense forest, and on the horizon were thunderclouds. Of course, this trip would have to happen right in the middle of the rainy season, she thought.

The moment Leslie's plane landed in Puerto Maldonaldo, she buzzed her contact in Nauta. The news came back that John had still not checked in. Leslie willed the passengers to disembark quickly.

The small airport funneled people out to the tarmac and then into the airport terminal. She grabbed her bags from the baggage claim and then noticed a familiar face hovering near the exit. She waived at Miguel, happy to see him.

"Miguel! Thank you for meeting me." They hugged as old friends. "Have we received all the equipment?" Leslie asked.

Miguel's smile faded just a little. Leslie mentally slapped herself for jumping right into business, but that was her way when she was readying herself for an expedition. Although, normally it was an expedition into a frozen tundra and she had her trusty guides and crew to work with.

Miguel nodded. "Yes. The equipment is here." The smile on his face was completely gone now.

Maybe it wasn't her abrupt turn to business that had soured his mood.

He reached out as if offering to carry her bags, but she waived him off.

"No thanks, Miguel. It's no problem. How have you been?"

Miguel's expression turned wry. "I've been missing my brother. Every time I go into the jungle to explore, I keep expecting him to wash the camp dishes after a meal. So, not only do I miss him, I really hate doing the dishes." He winked and then lead the way through the airport.

Leslie wondered if he was covering up his real pain, or had he really recovered enough to joke about his brother?

Miguel waved at a guard that had a rifle strung over his

shoulder, a standard for airport security in Peru. "Louis, I'm showing Leslie Kicklighter to the hanger."

The guard nodded and allowed them to pass through the door to the outside and back on the tarmac. Immediately the familiar feeling of sixty-five percent humidity clung to her skin. Luckily, the temperature being only in the seventies it didn't feel oppressive. Not like the ninety degree heat they would find in the Amazon.

"Miguel, is there something you're not telling me?"

He glanced over at her then his gaze moved off to the side. Leslie looked over to see a red-haired woman walking toward them.

Miguel made an exasperated sound. "*Maldita*. I'm sorry. I was going to tell you about her. She's been hovering around the airport waiting for you."

There was no time for him to say more.

Leslie turned toward the strange woman. Her inappropriate attire for their surroundings reminded Leslie of her friend Samantha Sorrenson. The red-head wore black leather pants, yellow cowboy boots, and a tight brown tank top. Leslie reminded herself not to judge a book by its cover.

"Leslie!" The stranger had a decided Russian accent and opened her arms as if going for a hug.

Leslie stepped back and out of the way of the hug, curling her lip in distaste of strangers trying to be too friendly. "Do I know you?"

The redhead brought one hand to her hip and the other to her chest. "Leslie, I'm sury. John's spoken about you so much I feel like I know you. I'm Anya."

"Anya?" Leslie wondered if she had met this woman somewhere. She did meet a lot of people at her various events. But she had never heard John mention an Anya, she was sure of it. "I'm sorry. I don't think I know you."

"Ve'll just have to have a talk with John about that. I'm Anya Vairue-Holbrook, John's vife."

Leslie felt her heart plummet to the ground. "Wife?" Leslie croaked out.

"Yes, that's me. So ven he talks about that battle-ax at home, I'm the one he's referring to."

"You're talking about the John Holbrook currently lost in the Amazon?"

"Yes. Miguel told me you're heading into the interior to find him. Although, he's not entirely lost. I put a tracker on him."

"Excuse me?"

Anya nodded. "He doesn't know, but I wasn't going to lose him again. I put a tracker on him. It's in his boot."

Leslie felt a little bit of anxiety slip away. A tracker would make a big difference in narrowing their search. "That's amazing. You can explain the tech to Miguel and I and we can use it to find him."

Anya's laugh was hollow, "Oh no. That tracker stays vith me. I'm coming vith you."

"What?" Leslie's left eye brow shot up. "What makes you think you can survive in the Amazon?"

Anya raised her head a little higher. "I am tougher than I look. I'm Russian." She shrugged her shoulders as if that fully qualified her.

Leslie could easily see Anya fitting in on a catwalk at a fashion show or maybe sitting in a bar in Russia ordering vodka watching old episodes of Friends on the TV, but not in the Amazon. "What experience do you have?"

"I've trekked through the Siberian wilderness many times. I know the hardships and the mental fortitude necessary for such a task."

Leslie raised her eyebrows. Mental fortitude was certainly something that was needed but the jungle was very different from a frozen forest. "Certainly you're not expecting to wear that into the jungle?" She nodded toward Anya.

"Of course not. I'm just being fashionable before I have to vear ugly jungle clothes. Listen, I have the tracker and you need me. Ven are we leaving?"

5

ONE MORE THING

Leslie had agreed with that they wouldn't take off without her. Although, Leslie wasn't convinced that Anya was as tough as she said she was, and had the urge to head out without her and the tracker anyway.

She'd find John one way or another in order to keep her promise, but after that she was finished with him. The tracker would help save them time, perhaps shave off days or weeks in their search, and might mean the difference in saving his life. She couldn't take the chance of losing him, even if she was mad as hell at him.

She stalked across the tarmac behind Miguel toward a hangar, wishing she could stow away somewhere and think about this new development. But her own timeline gave her no time for self-pity or despair.

As she had instructed Miguel, the equipment lay arranged on a tarp on the floor of a hanger, next to an eight passenger airplane. It would be carrying her, her team, and the equipment to their next stop, the Tambopata Research Center, where they would get the permits allowing them into the interior of the Amazon basin. Then a boat would take them to Nauta and on into the deep jungle from there.

There wasn't a big pile of equipment on the tarp, but then there shouldn't be. She and AJ had purchased the lightest and simplest equipment to get them through the jungle safely.

"Looks good. I'm glad I asked for extra backpacks, just in case. Are they here?"

He pointed to a large box. "They arrived a few hours ago. I haven't unboxed them yet. All the other equipment you asked for is here too." He had stressed the word equipment.

"Oh no. Please, don't tell me something else is wrong."

He sighed and said, "I hate to tell you this, but the pilot said that he can't fly you out tonight."

A hiccup. Something to be expected. She could deal with a small delay, but it grated on her need to stick to a plan. "How long before he can be ready?"

Miguel squinted as he replied, "A week, at least."

"Miguel, is this just the pilot's plea for more money?" She had seen resources drag their feet before in the hopes of bribes.

He shook his head. "No. At least, I don't think so. Actually, maybe it is, but he didn't tell me. He said he just didn't feel like working this week."

Leslie looked around the hangar. "This is his plane, right? Is he here?"

"No. I haven't seen him around for a couple of days."

She had a couple of hours before AJ would arrive and then they could leave. If they had a pilot. "Is there another pilot who could do it?"

He shook his head. "Sorry. He's the only private pilot there is from this airport. There's no other way you could arrange for a flight from here to the research center."

"Okay. Where do I find this pilot?"

6

IN THE MIX

Inside the lobby of her apartment building in the heart of
New York City, AJ Bluehorse waited. When her phone
beeped, it wasn't her Uber as she had expected.

It was a video clip from Frederick of the dogs, wagging their
tails as he told them to wish her well in the Amazon. Then he
turned the camera to himself. "Love you AJ. I wish I could go
with you, but I know that you're better prepared and ready for
anything this time."

AJ knew he was right, yet still wished he was able to come
with her. However, he was running a high-profile job for the
DEA. Besides, someone had to watch the bevy of dogs she had
collected before realizing her powers had been calling them to
her. The least Viracocha could have done was to give her some
instructions on these powers before leaving them to her.

She sent a heart back to Frederick at the same time she
received her Uber update that her driver, Mix, had arrived. She
walked out into the gloomy, cloudy New York day.

The driver had popped open the trunk, waiting for her

luggage. The man matched the image on her Uber order so she handed him her suitcase.

Their hands met and a sudden, jarring electric current ran up AJ's arm. The man jumped back from her, alarm written across his face. She assumed that he must have felt the electric shock, as well.

"Sorry!" AJ said. "It must have been some static electricity from all that dry air in the building." It was the best excuse she could come up with, having seen some static cracklings during winter time.

But there had also been a mental shock when she touched him. She had seen a flash of something in her mind, but it had gone away so fast that she wasn't sure what the image meant. She mentally shook it off and figured this was just another manifestation of her powers, given to her by an Inca god, that she'd have to figure out.

"No problem." He put her suitcase in the trunk.

AJ climbed in the back seat and was assaulted by the scent of candles. There were two candles, one sitting on the dash and another sitting in the middle of the front passenger seat. She wasn't quite sure how they would stay up while he drove. Or did he hand them to passengers?

He jumped in and started the car, pulling out into traffic with ease. She watched the tall glass containers with white candles continue to burn and not fall over as he turned toward the airport. She had an urge to reach out to touch them and see how they were staying in place.

Instead she asked, "What are the candles for?"

"Ambience. I'm Mix, by the way."

"Interesting name. Is it short for something?"

"Yes." He turned another corner and didn't seem as if he was going to answer. Then when he was on the highway he glanced into the rearview mirror. "From the app, I take it your name is A.J. Is that short for anything?"

Then she realized that she too was going to keep things simple, because she didn't want to talk about her real name. "Yes, it is."

"Hmm. Seems like we have a few things in common."

She stayed silent for a while as they continued toward the airport. She thought about her friend John and hoped they would find him alive in the jungle, but every day that went by made that less possible.

She used her phone to check her email, she had one from her cousin in New Mexico. She read it while Mix wove through traffic. Her cousin let her know that medicine man Darryl was doing well since getting out of the hospital and that he had asked about her. And that the rest of her family on the Navajo reservation hoped she'd come back to visit soon. That made AJ's heart feel warm.

Mix pulled into the covered area for departures and jumped out to get her luggage. As he drove away he waived at her and said, "See you later."

AJ did a double take. The words had translated in her head as English, but he had said them in some other language. And she had completely understood. Not only that, he had known she would understand.

When she got back to New York, she'd have to ask Annie, her Moon Cycle Coach, if she knew someone named Mix. Someone with powers like hers perhaps? Or someone ancient like Viracocha had been? Certainly those of the same nature as AJ had to be known to each other. Although, she didn't imagine there were enough of them to make some sort of club, and what would they call it if they did?

Humans with God-Like Powers? The Indigenous Powers? *Los Fabulosos*? She laughed at the thought.

Now though, she had to focus on getting to the Amazon and meeting up with Leslie. The sooner the better. They were going to cruise into the jungle, find John, and get out of there as quickly as possible. At least with Viracocha gone, they'd have less to worry about and maybe this trip would run more smoothly than last time.

7

TANGLE WITH THE PILOT

Leslie took deep breaths as the taxi sprinted from one lane to another. She appreciated the quick nature of Peruvian taxi drivers but would have loved more structure in their driving. She hung on to the front seat as he took a corner like a Nascar pro, then turned the other direction, bouncing her into the car door.

The taxi thankfully came to a stop. The driver, sunlight reflecting from his dark sunglasses, was smiling ear to ear, obviously enjoying his work. Whether that was driving, or torturing American tourists, she wasn't sure.

Leslie handed over the fee. "Can you wait here for a few minutes? If I don't come out in ten, go ahead and leave. I'll find another taxi at that point."

"*Sí.*"

She walked toward the house numbered 1141, the pilot's house. Miguel had given her his first name. David. She was looking forward to talking to this David.

As she knocked on the front door she heard the taxi take off. She shook her head. "Can't trust anyone these days."

The ranch style house was colorful with white siding, red shutters and a matching red front door. Two giant planters spilling over with pink bougainvillea were on either side of the porch. A warm, humid breeze waived through the branches.

The knock had not elicited any response. Then she heard splashing coming from around the back of the house. She followed the crushed stone path to the side gate.

"Hello! Can anyone hear me? I need to speak to David." No answer, but she could definitely hear the sound of splashing. She nudged the gate open a little and could see a swimming pool surrounded by green grass, with a few shade trees. In the pool, a man was swimming laps, oblivious to her.

She sat in the closest lawn chair and waited for him to finish.

He heaved himself up on the far side of the pool and grabbed a towel. While he stood facing away she admired the taught muscles across his back.

"I hope you don't mind. Your gate was open so I let myself in."

"That's because I left it open for you."

The voice. It was familiar. She tried to identify it, but was surprised when he turned to face her. "David Tafoya?" She smiled at seeing him. He brought back a lot of memories of climbing Mount Denali. They had been both been so young and naive about so many things back then. And the vacation they had taken together not long after surviving the dangerous climb had been one for the books.

"You knew I'd come here when I found out my pilot wasn't taking my flight today. What an asshole."

He laughed as he toweled off. "Is that any way to treat your pilot? I could leave you here with no other way to get to Tambopata Center and no way to pick up your permits."

Leslie rolled her eyes, but she knew that he was right.

He walked up and looked at her with his big blue eyes. "Aren't you going to give me a hug?"

Leslie jumped out of the chair and he enveloped her in a cool, wet, bear hug.

"What are you doing in Peru of all places?" she asked while his hands roamed down to her waist. She had a flashback of a long night in a cabin in the woods with David, curled up on the couch with a roaring fire.

"Waiting for you apparently," he cajoled as he slowly released his hold and stepped back to look her over. "I've missed you Leslie and those long nights in Alaska."

It had been ten years since she had last seen him, but he still looked as handsome and strong as he had back then.

"And since when are you a pilot? I thought you were aiming to be a doctor."

He shook his head. "I started into the college process, but it didn't feel right. My parents were happy to pay my way, but I wanted to keep adventure in my life. Flying planes in Peru is the closest I could get to it on a daily basis.

The tension of being angry at her "lazy" pilot was slipping away and she suddenly felt the weight of the long hours of flights. She sighed and sat in the chair. "Sorry. I'm a little exhausted."

"Exhausted, you say? That's weird. You just got here." His tone did not escape her.

"You did this on purpose, didn't you?"

He looked slightly sheepish at that. "Miguel told me about your trek. I know you want to find your friend, but killing yourself isn't the way. I figured, if I could get you here, I could get you to rest. Then you'll be ready for anything tomorrow. If you decide that you definitely want to leave today, I'm willing to go back to the airport. I'm not forcing this if you think you're ready to keep moving."

Leslie leaned back in the chair and considered. It was four PM Peru time. "How about a fourteen-hour break? AJ and I can get some restful sleep and get going first thing in the morning."

"Sounds good," David said.

"Okay." Leslie said, standing. "I'll get a hotel lined up."

"How about you set up AJ somewhere. I thought you could stay here with me. That is, if you want to reminisce about old times." His smile belied his interest in more than just talking.

Leslie smiled. "Oh. I see. You want me to rest, but you want to reminisce."

"So you'll get twelve hours of actual rest. Still a good deal." He looked sheepish. "That is, if you aren't involved with anyone. I didn't know if maybe you and John were a thing. Either way, I'd love for you to stay."

Her heart hurt but she needed to leave that behind and David was always at the right place at the right time when she needed him. "No, we're not a thing. He and I are just friends."

"Well, come inside and I'll make you a drink." David said.

She followed him in. The clean lines and simple design of the inside of the house surprised her. One entire wall was an image of the snow covered Mount Denali.

"Wow, it meant that much to you to get it as a wall?"

"I've been up Mount Denali six times. Each time it's been a new experience. That mountain does mean a lot to me."

Thinking back to her own climb up that mountain, she was glad that David had been there to support her as the only woman on the team.

She turned to him, taking the towel from his hands and throwing it on the floor. She took his hand and started toward the hallway, then realized she didn't know where she was going.

David took over at her hesitation. He led her into his bedroom, then turned and closed the door behind them while pulling her into his arms. "I've missed you, Leslie."

Leslie nodded. "I'm looking forward to getting to know you again."

He laughed. When his hand slid under her shirt and up her back, it sent a thrill through her. She relaxed into his arms, into his kiss, into his body. He wrapped his other hand behind her head, deepening the kiss and her whole body tingled.

Her knees grew week and he leaned her into a wall. She sighed with pleasure and he wrapped his hands around her waist, pushing up and under her shirt.

He stepped back to pull her shirt over her head.

He was growing warm under her touch as she ran her hands over his damp, naked skin. She could feel him getting hard through his thin swim trunks, his ardent interest pushing against her leg.

As he ran his hand down her legs, pealing off her pants, she unhooked her bra and tossed it across the room. He leaned back on the bed and pulled her down on top of him.

8

THE POWERS THAT BE

A J Bluehorse followed the exiting crowd from the airplane down a mobile staircase onto the tarmac. New York City had been humid when she left, rain pelting down as her plane took off, but this was even more so. If she was going to guess, it felt about seventy-seven percent humidity. At least it was a reasonable seventy-three degrees, and the sun was hidden behind soft clouds.

When she had checked the future weather in the Amazon, it was expected to rain the rest of the week and temperatures up to eighty-five and higher. She was already sweating in her light travel wear. Had it been an impulsive decision to come and help in the search for John? No, she thought, she needed to be here.

Besides, the powers from Viracocha felt stronger here, closer to its origins. Her reoccurring dream of walking into a gleaming Inca city had become clearer while she slept on the flight over. It felt as if she was meant to be here.

The crowd up ahead was filing into the small airport. As AJ waited in line to enter, she turned on her phone. Once inside, she headed for the baggage claim as her phone blew up with message after message. She sat in the first chair she could find so she could figure out the latest news. While she waited for her phone to catch up, she saw a man asleep in a chair getting his arms covered with Hello Kitty stickers by young girls sitting on either side of him. She hoped they were his own kids.

Frederick, Leslie, Samantha, and Miguel's names popped up in the message list. Frederick wanted to know how she was; her friend, Samantha was currently home in California and had sent some information on edible plants in the Amazon as well as an offer to help with anything, Leslie had let her know that they would stay the night in Puerto Maldonaldo; and Miguel had sent her the address of the one hotel in town.

She let Frederick know she had arrived at the final airport and was fine but tired; she thanked Samantha but said she hoped she wouldn't have to use the information and that she had an idea about what Samantha could do to help her and Leslie, if she was willing; she replied to Leslie that she was glad for the rest; and thanked Miguel.

It took a while for her bag to drop down onto the baggage carousel. Most everyone had their bags and were walking out as hers plopped down from the conveyer belt onto the carousel. The airport lights flickered and the carousel stopped, AJ assumed it was due to the sometimes unreliable electrical grid in this part of Peru.

A man, bent with age and holding onto a young woman's hand shook his head. "Why? Why does it have to happen with my bag. It could take them hours to get the electricity going again."

He was the last one left from the flight without his bag and there was nothing within view on the ramp. AJ made sure that no one was touching the carousel and sat down on the metal rail.

She sent a burst of electricity through it. The carousel jolted into motion and the ramp ran for a minute, just long enough to pull one more piece of luggage into view and drop it within reaching distance. The old man smiled and the young girl grabbed his bag for him. It wasn't much, it wasn't like when she had defended a homeless man in an alley from a threatening jerk, but it felt good to do something for someone with her powers.

As she walked outside to grab a cab, she reached out with her thoughts and was relieved that she didn't sense any darkness nearby, so no evil supernatural beings, at least that she could detect. The Twin Warriors of Navajo legend had warned her something evil was coming in the future; at least it wasn't around this airport and hopefully it wasn't waiting for her in the Amazon.

9

RESTLESS ENERGIES

After a taxi ride to her hotel, the Soy y Luna, and dinner at a local restaurant, AJ went back to her hotel room but her body wouldn't let her sleep. The energy inside her was swirling. It was like it knew it was close to home. When she did close her eyes, her recurring dream of walking around the ancient city of Viracocha's people would play out without her even being asleep.

She felt that there was something in her dream she was supposed to see but wasn't sure what that would be. She would always get close to the center of the city's gleaming golden stones and temples and fountains but her feet would stop just outside a building and not go any farther.

She stepped out onto the balcony that spanned the front of the hotel. Bright pink and orange bougainvillea hung from hooks all along the roof and brightened the gloomy view of the small city and not so distant jungle. Gloomy due to the torrent of rain.

Even in the rain, people were going about their business. She noticed that the sidewalks were raised off the ground to keep people out of the water that was running down the streets, and almost everyone wore rubber boots.

She had an urge to shout from the balcony and bring all those eyes gazing upon her. To reach her hands up to the sky and bring down the lightening like a spotlight. The feeling passed, and she realized that the god powers were getting to her again.

Thunder rolled through the street and although she hadn't seen the lightening, she had felt it. She grabbed her raincoat and threw up the hood, taking the balcony stairs, she joined the other stragglers out in the rain.

She was glad of her water proof hiking boots and they felt almost as comfortable to her as her old army style black boots she preferred. The feeling of power building in the air tickled her senses.

She reached out with her mind and could feel a lightning bolt building high in the atmosphere. Then the lightning struck a mile away, loudly thundering through the town. Around her people were walking and children were playing in the mud without a care about the electricity that boiled above their heads. They'd probably seen enough thunderstorms to not be worried.

Now though, she could feel the power building again and closer this time. Last week, she had been able to hold back an explosion long enough to let people escape the building. Could she hold back a lightning strike?

The energy was building quickly. She formed a bubble in her mind like she had with the explosion. She could feel the power of the strike pushing against the wall of the bubble.

The electricity wasn't dispersing, it was continuing to build so instead of holding it back she tried aiming it. She moved the bubble out and away from the town. The lightning struck about a half a mile away, so large the sound actually rippled through the rain puddles and everyone stopped to look. Many put their hands over their ears because of the loudness of the jarring sound.

The residents were safe, but AJ felt a huge surge of power inside her. It was as if she had absorbed a small part of that massive electric strike.

She walked down the street to the edge of the jungle.

She paused before walking in. She didn't know what she could do. She knew there was a possibility that she could burn so hot that she could tear down this whole forest. She would never want that to happen. Just last week she had melted steel by touching it. How could she release this energy that was pent-up inside her without damaging the people and the environment around her?

Her dogs had come to her in her need and had been able to syphon off some of her excess power. But here she had none of her lovable mutts.

As her hands began to glow she reached out with her mind to call out to anyone or anything that could help her.

She heard it before she saw it. Huge wings beating the air and a piercing warning cry was the largest bird she had ever seen descended to the forest floor, its wings a beautiful patchwork of black and white.

The face of the bird was like that of an eagle, but its head feathers were pointed up like a crown. It walked toward her on large taloned claws, its head just about reaching her at mid-thigh. At five feet away it stopped and bowed its head.

She had déjà vu. It was like a dream she had had of being the God Viracocha where the snake had bowed before him and he had reached out to touch it.

As he had done in her dream, she reached out and touched the head of the bird. Its feathers felt soft and thick. The glow from her hands diminished and she could see the glow of electricity being absorbed by the bird. It was also releasing some of that energy into the ground through its feet.

When she felt that the excess energy was spent, she stood back. The magnificent bird nodded once again, looked at her with its dark brown eyes then lifted off, the wind from its wings blowing AJ's short hair.

AJ realized she would have to try and figure out her own way of expelling her excess energy into the ground. She wouldn't always have a dog or a magical bird to help her out.

She also had a bigger problem. She was about to travel with several people that she didn't really know. More than likely they would come into a situation where they would need her powers, and even though she had a magical amulet from her Diné ancestors that protected her from prying eyes, they would probably figure out that she wasn't ordinary.

Luckily, she completely trusted Leslie and Miguel. But she had heard someone unknown was coming. Could she trust that person to keep her secret?

10

MORNING RESET

Leslie walked into the restaurant and took a deep breath of the local flavors scenting the air. She immediately ordered beans, rice, eggs and two coffees for breakfast and choose a table by the window. She wanted to enjoy this little town during her time here, before she was knee deep in mud with only a select few people to interact with.

The small restaurant was a mom and pop place, with a great reputation. David had suggested it for her and she was happy to take in some local food. Although it was early she was surprised that she had the place to herself.

AJ walked in and Leslie jumped up. She had to stand on her toes to give her tall friend a hug.

"AJ! I'm so glad you're here," Leslie said.

AJ hugged her back and nodded. "It's so good to see you too, Leslie."

"I ordered coffee for you." It was perfect timing as a woman walked from behind the counter with the coffee.

AJ ordered her breakfast then turned to Leslie "What time is our meeting?" AJ said.

Leslie glanced at her phone. "Right, I love that Samantha set this up. We've got about an hour before we need to check in, so plenty of time for breakfast."

AJ drank her coffee quickly.

"Tough night?" Leslie asked.

AJ nodded. "A little."

"I'm sorry. Miguel said that hotel is the only accommodations in town.

AJ shook her head. "It wasn't the room. I'm just feeling a little anxious."

Leslie took a sip of her coffee and nodded. "To tell you the truth, I'm surprised you said yes. I know that our last trek through the jungle wasn't your thing, but I asked you to come because I know I can trust you and you know what to expect when we go out there."

"I'm glad you asked. I said yes because I think I can help."

Leslie wanted to ask what that meant, but instead sipped her coffee. AJ's brow was creased and Leslie had a feeling that she needed to give AJ a moment to think about what she was going to say next.

While waiting for AJ, Leslie felt in a mood to reminisce. "I remember the first time we met, on the bridge of the *Toy of the Gods,* both of us looking out over the Amazon river and thinking we were going to have an easy time. I feel like we were very different people back then."

AJ laughed. "I'll say so. And that wasn't that long ago."

Leslie nodded.

AJ started, "Remember when— " but stopped as a man came from behind the counter with both dishes of food.

They thanked him and Leslie dug in. For some reason, she never loved black beans so much as when she was in Peru.

AJ took a bite of her food and watched the man head back

to the counter. She took a sip of water and continued. "Remember when we were all talking about the strange occurrences that happened? That we thought maybe the god Viracocha was giving us some of his powers?"

Leslie nodded. "Definitely. John was able to make a dress that fit me perfectly materialize out of nowhere; I lit up cave rocks; and you had that blue flame coming from your hands. It's too bad we couldn't have kept those powers. Maybe John would have gone into a different line of business and we wouldn't be here."

AJ leaned forward and set her hand on the table, a purple flame erupting from her fingertips.

Leslie jumped back from the flame and gasped. "What?"

The man at the counter turned to look at them and Leslie covered up by quickly picking up the coffee cups and walking over. "More coffee, please."

She handed the filled cup to AJ who held the cup in front of her where no one behind the counter would see. The flame that came from AJ's hand enveloped the cup, starting from purple then turning blue and then yellow. Once the coffee started boiling, the flame disappeared.

Leslie shook her head. "Wow," she whispered. "You still have the flame."

AJ nodded. "More than just the flame. The way Samantha described it, I can manipulate wavelengths like electricity, sound, those sorts of things." AJ shook her head at the question in Leslie's eyes. "Samantha doesn't know. I was just talking to her about certain things and she clued me into what my powers are doing."

"What?" Leslie couldn't help repeating. Seeing an angry god in the Amazon jungle was one thing. Having a friend who could manipulate wavelengths was another. "Who does know?"

"Frederick, of course. Couldn't go through all this without telling my boyfriend. My family friend Daryl, a woman I know in New York that happens to specialize in supernatural powers, and now you."

"I'm honored to be in the loop."

AJ leaned back in her chair. "It's not just that, although I'm glad that you know. On this trip I may have to use my powers. I have an amulet that makes it so that people don't see what me using my powers unless I want them to. But, in a close knit group, people are likely to figure out that I'm not exactly normal. I want your help keeping it from them, if possible."

Leslie nodded. "You have my word, I'll do what I can."

AJ eyed Leslie's necklace. "I see you've added a piece of jewelry to your look. Strange for you, especially for a hike into the Amazon."

Leslie ran her hand over the necklace. "Well, after a run in with a god, I figured that I might need some protection. I had a metalsmith make it for me after a great deal of research that led me to some dark corners of old, dusty stacks. I don't know if it will actually ward off god-like powers. Actually, maybe you can test me and find out."

"Oh." AJ grinned. "This should be interesting. I'll try the purple flame, it doesn't have much heat."

The purple flame crawled across the table and stopped an inch from Leslie's outstretched hands. Leslie could feel a warmth in her arms. "It seems like my necklace is keeping it back."

AJ nodded. "I wouldn't want to try the hotter flames, it's possible that the necklace doesn't ward off stronger magic, but I can feel a push back."

The flames ended and Leslie felt the warmth subside in her arms as well. "I just have to hope that if we run into anything, it has weak magic."

AJ shook her head, "I can't imagine what we could run up against. Certainly there's nothing else magical now that Viracocha is gone."

Leslie knocked three times on the wood table, "I hope we don't find out."

11

TAKEOFF

L eslie couldn't help feeling that this trip was getting off to a good start. Her necklace had the ability to push away some of AJ's fire capacity, they had set up a surprise for John, she had more coffee in her hand, and the equipment was all accounted for and being loaded. And David was here.

David was ensuring that the load was distributed evenly in the small cargo hold of the plane. He spoke with Miguel. "Let's put that bag on this side. We need absolute distribution, at least as close as possible. We have a full plane."

Miguel shook his head. "We should have one empty seat."

"I had someone call that needs a ride into the Amazon. He's joining us. The weight balance will be much better with six people total."

Leslie looked sideways at David. "I thought I had paid for complete use of your aircraft?"

He didn't look up from shifting equipment a bit more through the small door in the side of the airplane. "Read your contract. You have say over your equipment, but I have complete control over who flies in my plane." He stood back up and glanced her up and down. "I could kick you out, if I wanted to. But I won't." He winked at her.

She guessed it wasn't a bad thing. As long as they didn't end up waiting for this mysterious person to show.

David pointed behind her. "That could be him there with the tall woman."

Leslie turned and could see AJ walking across the tarmac, accompanied by a man. He was shorter than AJ, but then who wasn't? As they came closer, she could see it was the man who had been wearing the archeological t-shirt on the flight to Puerto Maldonaldo.

So maybe she would get to ask him questions after all. She still didn't see Anya anywhere, but then she wasn't going to be heartbroken if John's wife didn't show.

AJ and Miguel said their hellos while David went to talk to the newcomer.

Leslie was triple checking her list of equipment when AJ walked over to her. "Why are we taking this other person with us? Miguel said her name was Anya, but that was it."

"Well, she introduced herself as Anya Holbrook, John's wife."

"John's wife?" AJ's voice went high. "What? That can't be right."

Leslie nodded. "Yep."

AJ put her hand on Leslie's arm. "Are you okay?"

"I am." As she said the words, she realized that her time with David had indeed helped her feel better, even though she felt betrayed by John.

"Okay. If we find him and he's in one piece, you just say the word and I'll set his pants on fire."

They both laughed.

David came around the back of the airplane toward them. "Glad to see everyone's happy this morning. Everything is loaded, we just got Alex's gear stowed. Now, where's our last passenger?"

Leslie looked out at the tarmac. Still no sign of Anya. "We could really use the tracker information that she has on John, otherwise I wouldn't really care about leaving her here. It could save us days, maybe more in our search, which in turn means a shorter, safer time for us." But time was wasting while they waited for her.

Then they all spotted her. She had commandeered a security cart and was racing across the runway. She screeched to a stop and hopped out, grabbing her backpack out of the back seat.

"I'm so sorry I'm late," she said.

David moved to take her bag. "Thank you for packing light," he said. "We've got a full load this morning."

David loaded her bag and locked the doors to the cargo hold, then everyone climbed into the airplane. Leslie took the co-pilot's seat and everyone else piled into the back seats. They each put on headphones.

"Are these necessary?" asked Anya.

David shrugged as he climbed into the pilot's seat. "The engine can be a little loud. This way you all can talk to each other without yelling over the sound of the engine. Plus, I can focus on flying. If anyone needs to talk to me, you can switch to channel four."

David taxied the airplane out of the hangar, jumped out and did his preflight tests, then climbed back in and taxied them toward the runway.

They had been in the air about five minutes when Leslie

spotted smoke in the distance. "Is that a fire?" She forgot David couldn't hear her, but Alex responded.

"No. That's the Coropuna volcano, about two hundred and sixty miles from here and about two hundred miles from Nauta. A few of my contacts in Puerto Maldonaldo said that they've been having earthquakes and that the volcano has become more active in the last few days."

Leslie frowned. "Well, at least we won't have to worry about any lava reaching us. How bad have the earthquakes been?"

"Anywhere between a four and five on the Richter scale."

"Dang," Leslie said. Something to be aware of if they explored any ruins.

Anya spoke up, "I don't really know everyone here. Can everyone introduce themselves maybe? I'd like to know who I'm valking into the vilds of the Amazon with. I'm Anya."

"I assumed all of you were heading to Nauta for the eco-resort." Alex's voice had a Peruvian accent with a touch of British.

AJ added, "I didn't have time to tell Alex what we were up to. Everyone, this is Alex. He's a professor here to do some research in the Amazon. I'm AJ Bluehorse."

"And I'm Miguel."

Leslie felt a tap on her shoulder and Alex asked, "And who are you?"

Leslie turned and waved. "I'm Leslie Kicklighter. I brought most of them here to join me in searching for a friend of mine, lost in the jungle."

"Lost? That doesn't sound good. I'm from this area and I know that many people who disappear in the jungle are never found."

Leslie's heart dropped into her stomach. Partly from the comment and partly from the plane dropping a few feet from turbulence.

"Oh no. Ve'll find him," Anya said. "He's too stubborn to die out in that jungle."

Leslie didn't want to talk about John around his wife, and she definitely didn't want to acknowledge that this trip might be a wild goose chase. She sat back in the seat and looked out over the vast sea of green that lay before them. She imagined John in there somewhere, waiting for her to find him.

12

THE CENTER

A s they circled the landing field above Tambopata Research Station, also home to the Peru office for Amazon research, Alex asked, "This friend of yours, why are you willing to risk your life for him?"

Leslie felt like he had read her thoughts. "I don't want him to die out here, alone. His ancestor disappeared out here too. I don't want him to end up being a story that someone tells. No matter what's happened, I want to make sure he gets home alive."

"A powerful statement. I hope you can find him," Alex replied.

"Alex," started Anya, "vat are you looking for out here?"

"I'm looking for a particular ancient site of the Incas. If I find remnants of it, I'll bring a team of students out here next year to do some excavation work."

The wheels touched down on the tiny airport's runway. David put the brakes on and stopped them just a few feet from the building. It was obvious they didn't get many visitors here, but all visitors heading to the Amazon who weren't staying at an eco-resort had to stop here and pick up their papers, applied for ahead of time.

As Leslie climbed out of the airplane she grabbed her small pack. She figured that anywhere there was an office that could keep you from doing what you wanted, there was someone who was looking to get their pockets lined. She had come with extra money, just in case.

Besides the landing strip next to the research station, there was a single lane dirt road that emerged from the jungle and led up to the building. The office was also on the edge of a tributary of the Amazon. Two boats were tied up to a small dock. The building itself was a hut really. A round structure made in much the same way as other Amazon buildings Leslie had seen.

In her mind she pictured metal desks piled with paperwork and two hardworking people in button up shirts and bermuda shorts sitting behind those desks. She knew that often her expectations weren't reality.

Alex pointed at the palm fronds that covered the roof. "I'm always amazed and awed at how the ancient ways are often the best. That technique was first used over a thousand years ago by the Marajo. The leaves are perfectly formed to distribute the water."

Leslie shook her head and smiled, "Spoken just like a professor."

AJ chimed in, "Actually he reminds me of our friend Samantha Sorrenson."

Alex looked back at AJ, his eyebrows raised high in surprise. "The actress slash cover model?"

AJ nodded. "That's her. She's also got a great memory for facts."

Alex nodded and smiled. "Never thought I'd be compared to a famous actress. It's already an interesting day."

Leslie then Alex went through the front doors, two flaps of wood on hinges, and then through a mosquito net clinging together with magnets.

The room was dark. She didn't see any overhead lights. A tiny bit of sunlight was trickling in from the sides of a curtain covered window.

Something didn't feel right. Her eyes adjusted to the low light and she could see there was one desk, made of wood. The chair behind it was empty.

"Where is everyone?" she asked.

Alex looked over at the chair. "There should be at least one person here to cover the desk. I've been through here a couple of times. David usually lets them know we're coming since he's one of the few pilots that come out here."

Leslie noticed a back door, approached it cautiously and opened it. The first thing she saw was a generator, the second thing she saw was a man lying on his side behind the generator, facing away from her. She dashed up to the man with Alex right behind her. She meant to check the man's pulse but stopped— his shirt showed multiple bullet holes and blood had long pooled on the ground beneath him.

She gasped. "Why would someone do this?"

Alex's brow furrowed and for a split second she swore she could feel body heat coming from Alex in waves.

Leslie flashed back to the time when Sun, who was housing the god Viracocha, had been so angry that he had exuded heat. For a millisecond she had thought the same thing was happening with Alex. But then suddenly the feeling shifted and Alex shook his head in response to her question. Of course, he wasn't a god. He was just a man and she was standing in the sunshine in the Amazon. That was all it was.

Alex stepped back from the body. "This is Marlik. I've met him before, when I was doing research. It doesn't make sense.

We're too far away from any warring tribes. Unless it's some problem someone had with Marlik or perhaps this was something more deliberate?"

"Deliberate?" Leslie asked.

Alex looked at her. "It means that we aren't getting our permits anytime soon. Who knows for how long. We should go look at the equipment inside and see if we can call for help." He dashed back into the building.

Leslie knelt down and closed Marlik's eyes. He didn't look scared or surprised. She hoped he hadn't felt any pain. Then she walked quickly into the building to join Alex. From the light from the open door, she could see Alex holding the radio handset, and it had been cut from the radio.

"Damn," she said and walked to the front door. They'd have to call for help on David's aircraft radio. As she reached the door, the sound of gunfire ricocheted through the building. Alex jumped in front of her at the doorway and rushed outside.

Leslie was more cautious. She stayed at the edge of the doorway and looked around into the valley of the runway. David, Anya, and Miguel were taking shelter on one side of the plane. Another shot rang out and the distinct sound of a bullet hitting the airplane.

Leslie stayed low and walked around the building, finding AJ knelt down with her eyes closed. Leslie wondered if she was sending some kind of wave at the shooter, but wasn't sure what that would be. Would AJ risk sending fire? Alex stood next to Leslie, scanning the nearby jungle.

Another shot rang out. Howler monkeys suddenly filled the valley with the sound of their plaintive screams, like the sounds of a wind tunnel, a scary wind tunnel. Another shot rang out, but it sounded farther away. The next one even farther. A last shot could be heard coming from the jungle toward the other end of the runway. Definitely too far for anyone to be shooting at them anymore.

Leslie ran to the group at the airplane. "Are you all alright?"

They all nodded.

"What the hell was that about?" David asked.

Leslie shook her head. "I don't know. Someone's killed the clerk here."

"What!" David looked back at the building. "Shit."

"We need to use the radio on your plane to get the authorities out here." Alex said as he approached.

"Sure, once we take off, I'll radio for help. We can come back here once the authorities let us know they're ready for us."

Leslie crossed her arms and looked straight into his eyes. "David, I don't want to go back. It could take days maybe even weeks to get this sorted out. John doesn't have that time. They might even think we had something to do with the clerk's murder."

David leaned against the plane. "You obviously did."

Leslie's mouth dropped open. "What?"

"Look, I don't mean you killed the guy. I mean that someone must be after you, or Alex, or one of your other teammates. There's no other reason to kill the clerk and then fire at my airplane. Someone wants one of you out of the way. So yeah, they're going to investigate you all, I'm sure."

"David." Leslie looked internally for the calm she was seeking and kept her voice even. "John's life is in the balance. Besides, I doubt that person had anything to do with us. They must have killed Marlik and are just trying to cover their tracks."

David shook his head, "Look, I can't take the chance that my airplane will be hit again with a bullet. Plus, my livelihood depends on the good graces of the Peruvian government. I can't legally take you to Nauta without the proper documents. I'm lifting off with or without you. It's your choice." He leaned forward and grasped Leslie's arms. "I know your friend means a lot to you, but please, don't stay. Come back with me and have a little patience."

Leslie shook her head. Patience had never been her thing. Saving her friend, that was her thing.

Ten minutes later, Leslie, Alex, Miguel, Anya and AJ stood next to a pile of equipment and watched David's plane take off.

"David," Leslie said to no one in particular. "you really are an asshole."

13

ILLEGAL ENTRY

AJ shook her head as David lifted off.

Then Leslie pointed toward the river. "That's our way to Nauta."

Anya put her hands on her hips. "Vill this take us directly to Nauta?"

Leslie shook her head. "No. There are a lot of tributaries throughout the Amazon Basin and this one gets us close, but we'll have to walk a short distance. It would have been better if David would have been willing to take us without the permits, there's an airstrip there. Unfortunately, we have to make our way to the town because the river that John took is on the other side of Nauta."

Everyone grabbed some equipment and headed to the boats tied up on the dock.

As they got into the boats, a long, grey snake slithered into the river and disappeared under its murky surface. Great, AJ thought, a bad omen already. Not what I wanted to see day one in the Amazon. Although, did jungle snakes hold the same ominous power as a rattlesnake? She wasn't sure and it didn't matter— she wasn't turning back.

She choose to take the boat with Miguel and Anya. She hadn't had the time to get to know the redhead and if she was coming with them, AJ wanted to learn what she could about John's wife.

There were only two oars, so AJ sat in the back of the boat, watching Miguel and Anya push them off with the paddles.

"Let me know if anyone wants a break. I'm happy to help row."

She was hoping no one would ask. She hadn't taken the time to work out much. At least she was in better shape than the last time she had been here.

Anya was another matter. Her sleeveless shirt was showing off the muscles in her arms as she stayed in steady rhythm with Miguel's strokes.

"Anya, where are you from?" AJ asked.

"I'm a real estate broker in St. Paul, Minnesota. You?"

"Programmer from New York City."

Anya laughed and glanced back at her. "You vouldn't think a programmer or a real estate broker vould be in the Amazon."

Yes, AJ thought, but there's more to both of us than face value. Maybe it was the accent, heard in movies where Russians were so often the bad guys, that made AJ think Anya was more than just a real estate broker. AJ nodded and smiled back. "You're accent is decidedly Russian."

"Vat? Russian, me?" Anya laughed. "Yes. My sister and I moved here from Russia a few years ago."

The trees along the river were getting dense, many were right up to the edge of the river. She imagined that the trees had fought their way to the edge of the river for water and sun, but AJ knew the rainy season was flooding the river, raising the waters closer to the trees.

"Miguel, were you alvays an adventurer?" Anya asked.

He nodded and continued paddling, staying close behind the other boat. *"Si.* When we were kids, my brother and I camped out in our backyard and dreamed of exploring the jungles of the Amazon. Although, even with a child's imagination, I never quite imagined it as dangerous as it is."

Anya nodded. "Is your brother an explorer too?"

"He was. He died in the Amazon."

"Oh."

That conversation led AJ to the inevitable thoughts of how dangerous the jungle was. Of course, neither Miguel nor AJ were going to tell Anya that his brother had been taken over by a god and that's how he had died.

AJ asked Anya, "Did John talk much about Benedict Cecil Spafford to you?"

"No." The answer was curt, with a hint of don't-ask-me-more. Then Anya added more softly, "I found out a lot about John after he left." She paused a moment. "He had been going on a lot of trips and saying it was for his business. I retraced his steps on a trip to Washington DC and found he had been hitting the archives for research into Benedict and the search for gold. But he never told me about him."

AJ responded, "If it's any consolation, he never talked with his friends about it either. We didn't know that was the reason he decided to take his ship down the Amazon the first time."

"He told *her* though." The words were dripping with resentment.

Anya didn't have to say Leslie's name.

Then Anya added in a bright voice, "But I love him and I can't vait to find him and get him home."

The boat ahead of them was turning into a fork in the river. Miguel and Anya worked quickly to make the turn as well.

AJ's sigh was drowned out by the sound of the river, the paddles, the insects in the trees, and the frogs on the shore adding their calls to the universe. It seemed to AJ that this woman Anya was being driven by jealousy. AJ didn't think she could trust her. She would warn Leslie. The last thing any of them needed was to have to watch their backs from a fellow explorer.

A flock of bright green macaws flew overhead, their wings beating soft sounds into the air. She watched them fly away and wished she could experience the jungle the way they did— high in the trees, flying with the wind, and looking down on most of the dangers. When she looked ahead, Alex and Leslie were pulling onto a sandbar and it looked like they had arrived at their next destination.

AJ took a deep breath and steadied her energy and her thoughts. She had already helped the group once. She needed to be ready for the next thing, whatever that might be.

14

ROAD TO NAUTA

Leslie and Alex pushed off from the dock. Leslie was glad she had studied the maps and knew they should turn at the fork in the river up ahead. It was likely that Miguel also knew the way, but she had too much energy to hang back— she wanted to be the lead boat.

With every paddle dip into the water and out, she kept getting splashed. She looked over at Alex and he was moving smoothly, with no splashes of any kind.

"How are you not getting river water in your lap?" she asked him.

Alex glanced at her water-spattered pants and chuckled.

She shook her head and tried to imitate his movements but river water still swooshed into the canoe and onto her. She decided not to worry about it, at least the water was cool.

"Alex, my group and I are here for personal reasons, but aren't you worried about getting in trouble? I don't care if they never let me into the Amazon again, but you, you're doing research. It might affect your career."

ALEX SHRUGGED, "Maybe, but to tell you the truth, I don't want to wait. It took me long enough to get permission to get this far. I'd rather ask for forgiveness at this point. Where are you and your team going?"

Leslie hesitated. Everyone who was searching the Amazon for something was more than likely looking for gold. But Alex was a professor and a native, certainly he wasn't out to plunder or destroy his own ancestors' places. She decided to trust him.

"John was looking for the last resting place of his ancestor, Benedict Cecil Spafford. Specifically, the city of the Inca that worshiped at the pyramids we found last year."

Alex paused paddling. "Really? Then we might be going to the same place. I'm following up on some intel from a local who stumbled onto some ruins. He told me that he found a giant snake head, much like the one at the pyramids. Then he found some ruins, probably of a city."

Leslie remembered that snake statue and nodded. "Have you been to the pyramids? I thought my group and I were the first."

"No, I haven't been in person." He looked off to his left, not meeting her eyes. "I read your account about your trip in Adventure Magazine. I actually recognized you back at the LA airport, but I didn't want to act like some groupie."

Leslie laughed at the idea of having groupies. "That would be something. Adventure groupies."

He laughed with her.

Leslie tried to adjust the paddle again, her pants were soaked. She rolled her eyes when that didn't work. "Why are you out here by yourself? Shouldn't you be with a team?"

"It's expensive to bring a team out here. I'm sure you know that. Besides, I have to submit a pile of paperwork to the university, then build the team, then get through the equipment list. I don't want to do that unless I have proof. Besides, this jungle is the most dangerous place I've ever known. I want to make absolutely certain that a group trip can be as safe as possible. I wouldn't want to lose anyone on my team."

Leslie reflected on those feelings. She hated being responsible for other people. Though, knowing that AJ had powers made her slightly less worried; but certainly AJ was still susceptible to snake bites, attacking jaguars, and any number of things that could harm them. Miguel at least had a lot of experience in exploring the Amazon. And then there was Anya. Could she actually handle what the Amazon was about to deal them?

Alex stopped paddling again and looked at Leslie. "You know, I'm supposed to meet my guide in Nauta. Maybe we can travel together? At least until we figure out if we're going to the same place."

Leslie liked the idea of having other experienced locals with the group. She trusted Miguel, but she also knew the Amazon could be unforgiving and unexpected things could always happen. "I like that idea. How were you planning on getting down the river?"

"My guide has a boat waiting for us. You?"

"I purchased inflatable canoes. I did bring a few extra because I don't expect them to last in this environment, and we won't need them coming back. I expect to be able to take John's ship."

The fork in the river was up ahead, Alex and Leslie took the sharp left. She glanced behind to make sure the other boat was following and she felt the tension in her shoulders relax a little at seeing them easily take the fork.

The river carried them along. It wasn't long before Alex pointed toward the shore. "This is where we need to pull in."

They paddled and made it onto a sandy beachhead, obviously used often as indicated by a path leading up from the beach. They pulled their boats up on the beach, setting the paddles to the side.

Miguel pointed at the path. "That will take us to Nauta. It's about a twenty minute walk."

Leslie appreciated that Alex grabbed up one of their equipment bags. They had a lot to carry, even if it was only twenty minutes away.

She put her backpack on then secured one of the equipment bags on her front. Something she had done as a kid backpacking through Costa Rica when she had packed too much. If she could do it then, she could do it now, although this time she had packed exactly what they would need to get in and out.

Everyone else followed suit. Alex waited until everyone was ready then took off up the path.

Leslie's heart beat faster. Now there was no turning back and the jungle beckoned.

15

NAUTA

After walking the path through a few open fields, past the tiny airstrip that David would have taken them to if they had permits, then into the jungle, they finally came upon Nauta. The town consisted of one dirt road that led to the eco-resort, the locals homes constructed in the round fashion with palm fronds for roofs, a few businesses, and the dock. As they neared the dock, there was a cluster of boats pulled up on a sandy beach area, selling their wares to a group of tourists from the resort. And, even though she couldn't see it from here, Leslie knew there was a newly built school on the outskirts of the town— one that she and her friends had helped build.

The last time Leslie had been into Nauta, she had been impressed with the vendors in their boats, selling everything from earrings to edible ants. And when she and her fellow tourists had returned from their jungle adventures to Nauta they were all fast friends, after almost dying at the hands of a villainous drug lord and an angry Inca god. Back then, they had only been in the jungle a few days, but it had felt like forever.

Now, as they walked into the town, she felt almost like she was home. She shook that thought away. Once she got John out she was never coming back. This place wasn't home. It was just an oasis compared to the rest of the overgrown Amazon. If the jungle wasn't trying to stop you from moving forward, it was sucking you down.

Leslie spied the resort's shuttle van parked along the road. "I'd like to drop all this equipment at the docks and hop a ride to the eco-resort. I need to send a quick email, and they are the last chance for internet anywhere."

Miguel led them through the town to a building with a sign that said "Boathouse."

More memories flooded back. The last time she had been to the boathouse, she had been so smitten with Simon. Wow, she made terrible choices in men. Madman Simon Leverence the drug lord, David the unsupportive jerk, so why wouldn't John be married?

The boathouse was huge and very empty. Inside would normally be the *Toy of the Gods*, the state of the art ship that could traverse river and air. But because John had taken it on his trip, and his other version of the ship had been transported to Egypt for testing on the Nile, they'd have to use old fashioned methods. Hopefully they would be able to find the ship and use it to come back.

Leslie gladly dropped the bags and stretched out her neck and arms from the strain of carrying so much weight on her shoulders.

"Anya, this tracker system that you have on John, do you know for sure that it's working?" Leslie asked. She figured if they had any chance of getting rid of Anya this was it. If she had been lying to them, Leslie was going to leave her here at Nauta where she could at least get a boat back to civilization.

Anya nodded. She pulled out a square device that looked

similar to a cell phone. "It's a satellite based GPS tracking system, so it should be vorking." She played with some buttons then turned the screen away from herself. Leslie, Alex, and Miguel moved in closer.

On the screen was a map and a blue marker in the middle of a field of green. Without streets and other markers, it looked like nowhere.

Anya continued, "And ve can see his route that he took." She touched a button and turned it back around. There were a series of black dots connected with black lines. The first starting from the river, which was where he must have docked the ship before moving onto land.

"Can you pan out and show us our location in relation to that?" Miguel asked.

She nodded, pushed some buttons and showed the screen to everyone. The bigger view helped Leslie know what they were looking at.

Miguel nodded, "That looks right. So, we basically need to make our way down the river until we run into his ship, then move inland from there."

"What do you think the ETA to his boat will be?" Leslie asked.

Miguel shook his head. "We've already lost half the day getting to Nauta. If we can make good time today, maybe by late tomorrow we'll be at the ship."

Leslie sighed. It couldn't be helped and she needed to make that run to the resort.

Miguel pointed at the pile. "I'll start work on inflating the kayaks."

"I'll help," Anya said.

Alex moved toward the boathouse door. "I'm going to go find my guide. I'll be back here as soon as possible."

Leslie walked out with AJ by her side. They easily talked the shuttle driver into taking them to the resort.

As the van took the dirt road, AJ pointed behind them at the boathouse. "I just want to warn you. Anya definitely doesn't have your best interests at heart. It's hard to tell how much resentment she has, but she definitely has some jealousy towards you."

"Weird," Leslie said. "I don't see why." Although, Anya had obviously heard about her from John, or maybe it was that article in Adventure Magazine. She had written a lot of things about the captain and there was that picture of them standing close on the bridge of the ship.

When they arrived at the eco-resort, Leslie headed straight for the restaurant, the only place with electricity and the one and only computer with access to the internet. It was lunchtime and the place smelled like roasted meats and baked bread.

Leslie's stomach rumbled as she walked to the computer, thankfully available.

"Who are you contacting?" AJ asked.

"A certain senator with deep connections in Peru. I'm going to let him know what happened and have him start the wheels turning to help us."

"Ah, Devan. Okay. I'll be right back."

By the time Leslie had logged into her email, sent off a few messages, and logged off, AJ was back with a plate of food and a cup of coffee for each of them.

"We don't have time." Leslie said, feeling the moments ticking away.

AJ pointed her toward a table. "I need to do some of my own emails real quick, so you go eat and we can leave shortly. Besides, I'm sure everyone else is taking a break while they're waiting for us to get back."

Leslie dug into the plate of roasted beef, a slice of fresh

bread, and a piece of cantaloupe. By the time she was done AJ had finished her research, and her food as well, and had a bag in her hand. "I ordered some burritos for everyone. I figured it's something we can eat while on the river and that way we can keep moving until we start losing light."

"AJ, you're brilliant. Thank you."

She nodded. "I have my moments."

They laughed and went to find the van driver. It was time for the next step and Leslie felt her heart beating faster again. That feeling of adventure just around the corner.

16

INTO THE JUNGLE

L eslie and AJ arrived back at the boathouse to find that Miguel and Anya had reorganized the gear. Everyone's backpacks were neatly against the wall and the rest of the gear had been tucked away into the small spaces of the kayaks. Alex was waiting and ready as well. AJ handed out the burritos and they found space for them in their individual gear.

"Aha! I knew I'd find you here." The voice echoed loudly through the empty boathouse.

Leslie jumped a little. She turned to find a stranger standing in the doorway watching them. He wasn't wearing a uniform, as she would have expected a representative of the Peruvian ministry to be wearing; so he wasn't someone chasing them down from the ministry. In fact, he looked downright casual.

He was wearing an old army fatigue top in solid green. The pockets were bulging and full, the whole shirt a wrinkled looking mess. He had a cigarette hanging off the end of his fingers and he was wearing big, dark sunglasses over his chocolate brown face, an old army green hat sat askance on his black hair.

She hadn't heard any accent in his words, in fact he had sounded American. Then she realized that she did know him. "Wait," Leslie said, "you're Dan Draper. The journalist from Cincinnati. I recognize you from the American reporting seminar."

He opened his arms wide. "You bet. I've been following this story about John Holbrook. I know you're here to find him."

Leslie relaxed her shoulders, realizing she had been holding them tight as soon as he had spoken.

He continued, "I also know you have no permission to go into the Amazon and that I'm coming with you."

Leslie shook her head and put her hands on her hips. "The hell you are."

"Either that, or I go tell the ministry you're here and then you'll never find your friend."

Alex took a step forward. "That's an empty threat. At least it had better be."

Leslie placed a hand on Alex's shoulder to restrain him from doing anything drastic. She realized that under Alex's shirt was pure steel muscle. "It's okay Alex. I'm sure Dan has better things to do than die in the jungle."

Dan shrugged. "What's that guy going to do? Kill me? I don't think so."

Leslie shook her head. "No. What I mean is the jungle would kill you. All of us have experience in the jungle and we know what to expect. You look neither prepared nor in any shape to be making this journey."

"Pfff. Don't let the cigarette fool you." He threw it on the floor of the boathouse and stamped it out.

Leslie's jaw clenched. "We already have an extra mouth to feed with Anya. We don't have enough food for you too."

Dan reached outside the door and brought around a back-pack. It was an old army pack. It looked like it was completely full. "Got all the things I need right here."

Leslie nodded at it. "Empty it. Let me see what's inside."

"You're not really entertaining the idea of bringing this man vith us?" Anya asked.

"We may not have a choice. But first, I need to know that he's not going to starve, or take any of our food," Leslie said, her foot tapping while waiting for Dan to do as she asked.

Dan hesitated at first, then opened up the top of the pack and dumped it's contents out on the floor.

Leslie bent down and quickly organized the items into piles. Food, cigarettes and cigars carefully wrapped in plastic, pens, a notebook, sleeping bag, tent, cooking gear.

She picked up the cigars, as well as some of the cooking gear. "We'll share cooking gear, so this will save some weight, and no cigars. These aren't necessary and you'll need all your strength just to get the necessities to the site." She placed the discarded items on a table in the back of the room. "It will all be there when you get back. That is if you get back."

"Trying to scare me, little woman? If you can do this, I can do this."

"Little woman?" Leslie wanted to punch him, but thought better of it.

Leslie had had enough. "You know what? Never mind. Pick up all your things and go tell the authorities we're here. I don't need to deal with another asshole today." She picked up her pack and made toward the other door. The others followed suit.

Dan started in with pleading. "Look, I'm sorry. I didn't mean to be disrespectful. Honestly."

Leslie turned back around as she reached the door. "My friend is out there. I have no time for this."

Everyone followed her out the door and climbed into their

individual kayaks. Alex climbed into his small boat with his guide. There wasn't time for introductions. Miguel, leading the way, pushed off then started paddling down the river. The rest followed while Dan watched them from the shore.

AJ called from her kayak, "Thanks Leslie. I don't think I could have put up with him either."

Leslie shrugged, "Honestly, I figured we'd just leave him behind somewhere any way. Not on purpose of course, but He didn't look very fit, not the type to make it in the jungle."

The stream was carrying them quickly and the kayaks were small and fast on the surface of the water. Alex started up his boat's engine in order to keep up with them.

Paddling on the river felt almost serene— the rhythm of the paddles dipping into the water was a mantra. Although the engine of the boat covered up the sound of all the creatures in the jungle, Leslie could almost feel them watching. Or maybe it wasn't the creatures, maybe some tribe was watching them?

She shook off the feeling and kept paddling, hoping they'd make good time. Up ahead she could see white expansive thunder clouds against the blue sky. She closed her eyes for a second and imagined John alive and well. "We're coming John. Hang in there."

17

RABIN

R abin watched the group slide by in their boats. Too bad she had used up all her ammunition. She got up and hobbled to a boat moored on her side of the river, dropped in her bag, and carefully pushed off. She knew she'd be a bit behind her quarry, but she'd catch up. She hadn't lived all these years in the jungle to be outsmarted by a bunch of tourists and one evil son of a bitch.

She set her injured leg up on her bag. The unusual chase and attack from the tiger had slowed her down, but now she had meat to cook tonight for dinner. Somehow, she was sure that Alex had to be behind the strange behavior of the tiger, but she had never known him to exhibit such powers. Perhaps he had found a way to add to the powers he already had.

If she caught up to these upstarts, she'd put them out of their misery quickly. But her ability to surprise him was gone. He'd know she was out here and ready to do anything to stop him.

The day she and Alex had met, she had been so young. She

had traveled to a nearby village with her tribe's shaman, to learn from a healer that was helping cure a sleeping sickness.

"Alex Quispe" he had introduced himself. "I've come back to bring hope." His words were in her language. That in itself had been a surprise. No one had met this young man before, yet he spoke their language. He looked much like them, but his clothes were like the whites that came to visit once and awhile.

That night, he came and sat next to her at the cooking fire. "Rabin, you have a special energy about you."

She nodded, scooping some boiled yucca into her hand. "That's why I'm being trained as a shaman. I have some abilities that others don't. Most think I have been blessed."

"Most?" he asked.

"There are those that think I have been cursed."

"And what do you think?"

"I think that I would not have my special abilities if the gods didn't want me to have them. So, I use them for what I can and what helps my village."

He stuck his bottom lip out, a sign of agreement used by her tribe. "How do you use them?"

"In the morning, I send my soul out into the fields to look for animals and let our hunters know where they can find good hunting. I can do it without sending my body. My soul can glide on the air."

"That's a great ability to have."

"Yes, but even if I find a hog, I will send them to where I find monkeys instead. I like monkey meat better."

He laughed, and his laugh made her own heart feel light.

It wasn't until years later, after she had taken him as her husband, that he had admitted he had his own powers.

Lying in bed, looking up at the fronds on the ceiling, she had wondered out loud, "Alex, why is it you never seem to age?"

"When I reached thirty, I stopped aging. It was around that

time that I discovered my own abilities. I have super human strength and endurance. I can also project illusions when I want to."

She sat up in bed. "But, you've never used these abilities?"

He had turned to her. "Rabin, I've lived a long time and I've gone through many seasons of my life. My first thirty years, I call those my normal years. I lived with a very kind family. When I turned thirty and began to manifest my abilities, they told me that I was the human son of Viracocha and his wife, the goddess."

"Since then, I've traveled the world, I've raised my own armies, and took on many enemies. I've watched battles rage with handheld weapons to metal fruits that fall from the sky and explode around people."

Rabin gasped. The image of metal balls falling from the sky was terrifying. And Alex had lived through all of that? She ran her hand over his face. "Gods, Alex. You have so much you could teach the world. Why are you here?"

"Well, I have you, don't I?"

But there was something else in his eyes, so she used her powers of persuasion to get him to tell her more. She weaved the words and the spell together. "There's more you aren't telling me. What is it?"

He lay back. "Yes. I've been thinking a while about a plan. More than running an army. I want to run the world. Viracocha had a staff, imbued with powers. I think that if I could find that staff, I could create my own gods. Gods to follow my path and help me rule the world."

Rabin was still for a moment. Certainly that couldn't be what her Alex was planning?

He continued, "I came back to the jungle to make my way to the old city and find the staff. I used my powers to cure a few things here and there to get help from locals, but I found you. My plans have no timetable."

Over the next few years, she tried changing his mind— but he told her that once the villagers chased him out for never aging, or when she died, whichever happened first, he would continue with his plan.

One night she had laced his drink with enough poison to kill an elephant.

After drinking, Alex sat quietly for a little while, seemingly unaffected by the poison, yet still aware of it. He turned to her. "Would it be so bad for me to be in charge of the world? Haven't I been a good man?"

Rabin wiped a tear from her eye. "You have, but power corrupts, and these magic powers can increase that corruption. If you took over the world you'd no longer be the same man I fell in love with."

Alex shook his head. "I've lived for so long Rabin. I don't think I'm like any man you've met before. What makes you think that I can be corrupted?"

She sat on the log by the fire. "My grandfather met Viracocha."

At hearing the name he turned toward her. "What?"

"He used to tell a story of meeting the god in the jungle. He would appear sometimes as a large red snake and other times as a chieftain. He once sat with my grandfather and told him of the stories of what happened before the Spanish came. He told him that at his highest point of command, when he had almost all of Peru at his command, he wanted more. He planned to take the world, and that he would have sacrificed all of his people to do it. That the hunger for power was almost too much. I think this could be in you, as well."

"So, you think I am my bastard father? His power was taken

from him long ago, mine is just beginning." With that Alex was gone, disappearing into the jungle.

That was when she knew she had to find him and finish him some way. If it took cutting off his head, she'd do it. She didn't think the world needed more gods or someone ruling over them.

She had also decided that anyone with Alex must also be her enemy.

She cursed Viracocha and spit into the river. This was his fault. Leaving an abandoned son with partial powers to find his own way in this world. It was his fault his son had strayed onto a dark path.

What she couldn't understand was why Alex hadn't already obtained the staff of Viracocha. He had been to the jungle and had found the city, yet he had left without the staff. Now he was back with more people. Did he need their help in some way? Maybe he hadn't been able to find the staff and now had the help he needed to find it?

But it also meant that she had this one last chance to stop him before the world was in grave danger.

As she paddled, Rabin glanced at the wrinkles on her hands. She had grown so old, it had been many years. All those years ago these hands, this body, this heart had loved Alex and she was sure he had loved her.

Then she felt her determination grow. She might be old, but she was resolved that he would not complete his plan.

She paddled harder, more resolute to do what must be done. She would destroy him and his supporters, even if it meant setting the whole of the Amazon on fire.

18

THE UNEXPECTED

L eslie glanced back to check on the rest of the group. So far, so good. The river pushed them along at a quick pace, gliding past trees roots and vines that touched the high water, colorful birds preening in the trees, and monkeys jumping and climbing from tree to tree.

She used her paddles once in a while, but they were more necessary for steering than for paddling.

Alex and his guide had kept their boat near Leslie all day. When the water was wide and calm, Alex would get close enough to toss a question over to her or start a conversation. When she pulled out her burrito to eat, Alex brought his boat close to hers and offered her a canteen.

She waived it away. "I've got my water."

He leaned over the side of his boat. "Seriously, you should try it."

She took the offered canteen and took a drink. She smiled at the taste. "Is this grape Nehi?"

He nodded.

She took a long drink of the fizzy, sugary liquid then handed the canteen back. "Got any more surprises?"

He laughed, "Always. But that's the only 'extra' food item we brought."

She was in mid-bite when she spotted something across the river up ahead. She set the burrito on her lap and got out her paddle. The blue reflection of the sky ahead was broken by a dark brown expanse.

She used her paddle to slow down her forward motion. Luckily, the others were paying attention too. Alex turned off his motor and the others slowed down as well.

One of the giant trees along the river had fallen in and was blocking their way.

"Make for the shore!" she yelled, glad that Alex had turned off the motor.

Leslie paddled hard toward the shore. The current was carrying them fast and if they didn't act quickly they would be moored on the tree or stuck in a whirlpool caused by the current and the blockage. The chance of damaging the kayaks, loosing equipment, drowning, or meeting up with a caiman were all abundantly possible.

She focused on the shore, pulling hard, and hoping that everyone was following suit. She heard Alex's motor start up. She wasn't really worried about him. With the heavy boat and the motor he'd be able to make the shore in time.

It was everyone in the kayaks that flashed through her mind as she struggled against the current and saw the blocking tree getting closer. She wasn't sure she was going to make it, the tree was coming up faster than the shore. She pulled harder, feeling her arms and shoulders take the burden of the stress.

Then the tree loomed large and she knew she wasn't going to make it.

Alex's boat swooped in front of her and cut toward the shore.

She pulled back on her paddle, trying to turn the kayak so she'd hit his boat sideways. The kayak slammed into the side of the boat.

Alex reached out and grabbed the mooring hook on the front of the kayak, his arm muscles looking like steel ropes.

His guide cut the motor and both vessels hit the beach, a mere foot from the seven foot diameter tree.

Leslie looked back. Everyone else had made it to shore and all were watching her. She did a thumbs up to let them know she was okay.

Alex leaned over his boat, watching her.

She shook her head. "Alex, are you okay? That was some stunt."

He nodded. "What about you?"

Leslie gingerly moved around and climbed out of the kayak, checking that everything was in one piece. "I seem to have lost my burrito, but otherwise I'm perfectly fine. I do feel like I just took a ride on a wooden roller coaster though."

"I'm not surprised. I'm glad it worked."

Me too, she thought. This could have been really bad, for her.

Alex patted his guide on the back. "While we have a moment, I want you to all meet Benignio. He's my guide and an old friend."

There were a quick round of introductions, then AJ pointed at the tree.

"Now what?" AJ asked.

Leslie considered their next step. Going around the tree would require them to walk all of their equipment, four kayaks, and a boat into the jungle, around and over mud and vines. To get over the seven-foot high obstacle would require something else. "I say we break out our axes, create some steps in the tree, and do a fireman's carry to get everything over the tree."

Anya was standing with her hands on her hips, looking at the tree. "Can't ve just make camp here tonight?"

Leslie shook her head. "We have about three more hours of daylight. I want us to get as far as we can. It might take us an hour to get over this obstacle, so that's two more hours of moving in the right direction."

Miguel was the first to reach the tree with his axe. "I've got this. Everyone else can start lining up the equipment for the trip over."

Leslie helped the rest of the group to get the equipment lined up for carrying over the tree while Miguel and Benignio took turns with the axe.

Anya wondered off toward a giant fig tree, looking up at its height. Suddenly, she screamed and stomped. Leslie saw several black scorpions climbing up Anya's boots.

"Come towards me Anya." Leslie knocked the scorpions off of the redhead with her hat. "Turn around." She knocked another one off from the back of Anya's pants. "Ok. I think you're clear. You must have walked into a sleeping group of scorpions."

Anya stomped some more. "Uck! I hate things vith too many legs. And scorpions, they have too many legs." She stopped, looking out over the river and pointed. "Vat is that?"

An oily black caiman was laying on the other side of the river, sunning itself.

Leslie wasn't happy to see one so close. "That's a caiman. It's the angry cousin of the alligator."

"Uck! I think I hate it too."

Leslie nodded. She wasn't a fan either.

AN HOUR LATER, they were ready to push off again. The boat had been a little harder to get over the tree, but with everyone lending a hand, they had safely gotten it over with no damage. As Leslie climbed into her kayak, she lamented the loss of her burrito, but the loss wasn't bad as things go. They all pushed out into the river, letting it take them along again. The brown river reflected the blue sky, and the white storm clouds. They were in for a storm tonight.

19

UNINVITED VISITOR

Time slipped by while they paddled, gliding on the top of the water. The storm clouds were growing and the sun was dipping below the clouds. Anya waved at Leslie and pointed toward shore.

She nodded and they made their way to the shoreline with the group following behind.

Leslie had already given everyone their job for camp. Leslie quickly put together a fire and set to cooking dinner; Anya and AJ set up tents; Alex and Benignio collected enough firewood to last through the night; and Miguel checked over the kayaks for damage and ensured they were ready for the next day.

Leslie pulled out the ingredients for tuna and noodles with powdered cheese.

When they finally sat down to eat, the camp was set up and Leslie was proud of the team. Anya might not like her, but she was taking orders and getting things done.

While Leslie was cooking, Miguel had cut up some small logs that he and Alex placed around the cook fire so that everyone could sit a bit more comfortably.

Exhaustion was evident on everyone's faces. Once they had a bowl in their hands, everyone dug in and focused on the food. Leslie thought the tuna and noodles was passable, but more importantly it had the nutrients they needed. It was a bit salty from the chicken noodle soup, but they'd need that salt to replace what they had lost today.

Her arms were exhausted from all the paddling. How she missed the *Toy of the Gods* and its fancy cabins.

Out of the corner of her eye she saw movement among the tents. "I think we have a visitor."

All eyes turned in the direction she was looking. A yellow and black snake was slowly making its way toward Alex's tent.

"Whoa," Alex said and leapt up, walking towards the snake. "That's a Bushmaster."

"Is it poisonous?" AJ asked.

"Definitely," Alex answered. "Which is a shame because it's also a rare snake to see and so beautiful. Look at that coloring."

Leslie got up and walked a little closer. It was a beautiful creature. The dots of yellow and black were lovely. But, it was still a snake.

Alex grabbed a stick lying next to him. "Can someone grab a machete? Unfortunately, we'll have to kill her. Otherwise she's just going to come back here and end up biting someone. Plus, she isn't acting aggressive now, but as soon as I'm seen as a threat she's going to get angry and start lashing out."

He calmly picked the snake up by its tail and used the stick to pic up its other end. It was easily six-feet long.

Leslie squirmed a little, glad that it wasn't reacting yet. She could just imagine Alex getting bitten. She grabbed her machete, something she had made sure to pack.

Alex lowered the snake's head back to the ground.

Miguel approached with a forked branch, small enough to

hold down the snake's head. "I'll use this to hold her while Leslie takes that swing."

The snake seemed to know what they were talking about. As Alex moved slightly to allow for the branch to hold her down, the snake tried to break away from Alex's hold.

Miguel slammed down the branch over her head, but even as Alex backed away and Leslie moved in, the snake was working its way out of the forked branch. Leslie raised the machete at the same time the snake pulled out of the hold. It rushed at Miguel's legs just as Leslie slammed down with the machete right behind the head. The body continued to writh a bit more before finally coming to a stop.

Leslie breathed a sigh of relief.

Alex took another stick and used them both to pick up the head and tossed it into the river. "I've seen a severed head bite a man's hand off once."

He picked up the body. "This will be a perfect breakfast tomorrow morning."

Other than the constant mosquitos that kept up an unceasing dance, Leslie hoped that the snake would be their only visitor tonight.

20

FIRESIDE

The sun slipped behind the horizon just as thunder erupted a few miles out. Leslie could see a group of bats flying along the river. She was glad to see them fly on, hopefully they weren't vampire bats. Or worse, magical vampire bats that could turn to human vampires. She shook her head, she didn't need crazy ideas in her head. This jungle was dangerous enough without magic.

Everyone else was mesmerized by the fire light.

The air was warm, about eighty degrees, but the light from the fire felt comforting like a touch of home while surrounded by the sound of millions upon millions of bugs, and amphibians, and birds, and other animals.

Everyone was quiet watching bits of ash rise in the air over the fire.

Alex nodded toward the flames and took a sip of water before saying, "There's a myth of the people of this land that at one time the condor's feathers were completely white."

All eyes turned to Alex.

"One day, the white condor came into a valley and spotted a

beautiful woman tending her sheep. He fell in love with her and decided he must have her for his wife. He turned himself into a man and walked up to her, asking her name.

"'I am Urpi,' she replied.

He talked with Urpi all day, getting her to trust him. When she was close enough he turned into the condor and carried her away to his nest high in the Andean mountains. She liked the condor, but she missed her family and wanted to leave, so she called out to the god Viracocha and asked for help. He turned her into a dove so she could fly home and escape the condor.

The condor was distraught when he discovered that Urpi had left his nest. He saw a fire burning in the forest. He flew down, planning on flying into the flames and ending his life, but Urpi saw him and called out to him. She told him he was a great leader and told him he must live for the good of his people.

He decided then not to kill himself, but still distraught, he went to where the fire had already burned the forest and used the coal to cover his feathers, forever making the condor black. He left his white collar so that the world might remember him in his beautiful and happy state. In his despair he also tossed the ashes into the air. So when you see ashes float, it's the great condor pining for his lost love."

Leslie could almost see a condor bent over the fire.

"That is a beautiful story," Anya said.

AJ raised her water canteen at Alex. "I'm honored to hear your ancestors' stories."

Alex returned the salute with his own canteen. "Care to share one from your own stories? Maybe one about skinwalkers. I'm fascinated by dark magic."

A peel of thunder in the distance punctuated his comment. It was definitely going to rain tonight.

AJ shook her head. "Maybe later."

Alex nodded. "By the way, I've been thinking about that person that shot at us today. Maybe someone is out to stop one of us from finding that city."

"What could be so important about the city?" Leslie saw Alex's eyebrow shoot up and she shook her head. "Look, I know it's a huge historical find, but why would anyone stop us unless they wanted to find it themselves. And if they wanted it themselves, they didn't need to wait for us to get there. They could already be there making the find."

Benignio shrugged. "Maybe it's a local who doesn't want anyone to ever find it, to protect it. There are many Peruvians that are serious about protecting old sites. Maybe that's why you haven't heard from your friend, John. Maybe they stopped him from finding it too."

"I definitely think we should be vigilant," Alex said.

Miguel finished his second helping of dinner and pointed around with his fork. "We should post watch tonight."

Everyone was in agreement. To keep the watch dry and the fire going, they put up a tarp above the watch area. Then everyone headed to their tents, knowing that they would each take a turn. Benignio was taking first watch.

Alex was heading the same direction as Leslie. She said to him, "Thanks for sharing that story. I'm glad you're here with the group."

He nodded. "Me too. Thanks. Sleep well."

At her tent, Leslie knocked a tarantula off of her doorway, hoping that Anya wouldn't see it. Leslie crawled into her one person tent, zipped up the doors, and laid back with her sleeping bag under her and a light sheet over her. Then the rain started. The sound of it tapping on her tent quickly lulled her to sleep and she drifted off dreaming of floating on a serene river.

21

THE GLEAMING CITY

AJ pulled off her boots and set them in the foyer of her tent, stuffing her dirty socks in the top to keep out spiders and centipedes. She pulled her feet into the tent and zipped up the door.

She didn't like that there had been two bad omens in one day, but one had to expect snakes in the jungle. Her auntie would have said for her not to ignore the omens, but what could she do? There was no turning back.

And Alex asking about skinwalkers had made her skin crawl. He didn't know that would bring up memories of her recent trip to New Mexico, but the battle with that evil witch had been hard on her— especially seeing her boyfriend incapacitated by the skinwalker.

She sat cross legged and breathed out the negative, as her yoga videos had taught her. She waited until she felt the stress melt away and then laid back.

She was glad the rain was pounding loudly against the tents because if she made noises in her sleep, no one would hear. If she glowed bright yellow while she slept, as Frederick had told her she had done a few times, that could be explained away with her lantern. She had made sure to bring one that had a yellow filter. She knew she would dream, which seemed to lead to her unusual nighttime activities.

She was sure it was due to being this deep in the Amazon, where her powers had first been born through Viracocha. Plus she could actually feel the dream calling to her. Sometimes her dreams were of people in trouble, but lately they had all been about the lost city in the Amazon.

She got comfortable and closed her eyes. Immediately she was in the dream, walking through the forest, her bare feet stepping on smooth stones. Ahead, was the entrance to the city. A group of white llamas were penned together inside a low fence, dining on the green grass.

She walked the road up to the walls of grey stone that surrounded multi-story grey buildings. Hundreds of residents were walking along the streets. Just like all of the intricate Inca stone work done in all their cities, and villages, and worship centers, the stones here were chiseled into shapes that fit perfectly against each other.

She followed the street downward into a square. In the square, the sunlight glinted off of a bright gold fountain with a jaguar's face spitting water into a large bowl. The water flashed with reflected light.

The building behind the fountain also shone with gold. Her eyes were attracted to the fountain but her feet wanted to take her somewhere else. She continued down the street to a set of stairs. She walked up the stairs and when she reached the top, which was shaded by an arching stone roof, she looked back at the valley.

Roads led away from the city in all directions, connecting the great Inca empire across the lands, from ocean, to mountain, to hidden inland cities. Her empire was vast and powerful and she stood taller with pride.

But she had somewhere to go so she walked down the other side of the stairs, then made her way to a small, nondescript building. The road here was well worn from thousands of feet coming and going.

She walked into the building, reached for another door, and suddenly a clap of thunder woke her.

AJ lay there assessing her dream. It was the first time in her dream that she had made it that far. Also new was that she had felt Viracocha's thoughts. But something important was in that small building, and she didn't know what. Maybe that was where they would find John? Though she doubted any of those buildings were still standing. The pyramids they had explored last year had been in decent shape, but they had been solid structures. The buildings in the city were hollow and, as far as she knew, not being taken care of by anyone.

She pulled out her lantern, a pen, and a journal that she kept for her dreams and wrote down everything she remembered, then tucked it all away.

The thunder clapped again and she saw the flash of lightening brighten the night even through her tent. The rain was pouring down hard like it always seemed to do here. No gentle rain ever seemed to fall. It was always raining giant cows, because, as Leslie had said once, cats and dogs just didn't describe it well enough.

But that was the way of the Amazon, it was grand and great and terrible. Nothing here was insignificant.

AJ took a deep breath and closed her eyes. She hoped if she dreamed again she'd get to see what was in that building, but she didn't hear the dream calling, just the fatigue from the day. She drifted off and dreamt of a crackling fire and hot chocolate on a cold day in New York.

22

PIT VIPER

AJ woke at first light. Her stint at the fire having been in the middle of last night's rainstorm. She was surprised that she was awake so early. She glanced through her journal to add some more notes about her dream, then got dressed and opened the tent, welcoming the cool seventy-degree morning temperature and the breeze coming from the river.

A flock of birds flew overhead and she wondered where the giant bird was that she had called to her during the other rainstorm. She had found out from her research at the eco-resort that it was a harpy eagle.

The sun inched up the horizon while she completed a few yoga poses that she could do standing, since the rain had made the grounds more of a marsh. She focused the energy in her body, an energy that pulsed in an aurora borealis color.

The struggle over the last months to make this power her own had been long, but now she felt the power was truly hers. She focused the power to move through her slowly, then used it to scan around her.

AJ's eyes shot open and she physically recoiled as well as retracted her energy. It was as if her mind had touched a spider. "AJ? What's going on?" Leslie was standing near her, concern mapped on her face.

"I- I'm okay, I just felt a darkness. It was like touching, I don't know, something that was wrong."

"Maybe that person that shot at us is out there somewhere," Leslie suggested, glancing out toward the inky darkness of the jungle.

Alex came out of the jungle, holding a canteen. "Everything all right, ladies?"

They both nodded. AJ thought about what the Twin Warriors had told her months before, that there was a darkness that was coming. That she would be needed to put a stop to that darkness. In Viracocha's memories, the darkness that made him recoil was the thought of the Spanish that had laid waste to his empire. AJ didn't know what or how vast the darkness would be. That felt overwhelming and humbling— and more than likely that darkness was greater than just some shooter bent on stopping them in their quest.

"Maybe," she responded to Leslie.

AJ would try it again tomorrow and see what happened. Right now, she wanted to get that dark feeling out of her mind. She closed her eyes again and instead of scanning for anything, she imagined a calming and peaceful place. She found herself back in New Mexico, standing in a desert looking over a painted valley.

At least in the Amazon, with all the humidity, she worried less about setting the place on fire with her powers. And with that thought she was back in the Amazon again. She gave up on trying to meditate.

Alex was at the cook fire, preparing the snake. AJ could hear him and Miguel arguing over the best way to cook it.

Miguel wanted to add some Cajun seasoning that he had brought, but Alex was insisting that "the simpler the recipe the better."

AJ would never eat snake, it was bad enough that she had to see them around her. The closest she was willing to eat was the caiman from last year, which had been okay. But then, her normal meals consisted of heading out to the corner sushi bar or ordering pizza delivered.

She went back to her tent and packed up everything, knowing they would be leaving as soon as humanly possible. When she was done, she moved her things over to her kayak.

Everyone else had broken down their gear, but there was one lone tent still up. Leslie was walking toward it and yelling "Anya!"

Alex announced, "Breakfast is ready!"

AJ reluctantly walked toward the fire, hoping there was something more than just snake to eat.

23

TRAGIC STORIES

L eslie felt that the morning was moving smoothly until she realized that Anya hadn't even gotten out of her tent yet. She dashed over,.

The groggy sounding voice from inside the tent at least told Leslie that Anya was alive. From her own experiences, Leslie wouldn't have put it past the dangers that lurked in the Amazon for Anya to have disappeared without a trace.

"Vat time is it?" The question came from inside the tent.

"Time for you to get up, get packed, and maybe eat some breakfast if there's any left when you're done." The threat of no food seemed to work. Leslie could hear the sounds of someone slinking out of a sleeping bag.

Leslie headed back to the fire with her meal kit ready. She was looking forward to trying the snake. As she approached, she took a deep breath of the smell of bacon and smiled. Alex indeed knew how to do breakfast right.

She spooned up eggs, bacon, a few pieces of snake, and poured herself a cup of coffee before sitting down with the rest of the team.

Miguel had a piece of snake on his fork.

"What do you think?" Leslie asked him.

Miguel took a bite, had a few chews, and nodded. "It's like bland fish. Not much flavor. Which is why Alex should have added the Cajun flavoring, but it's not bad as snake goes." He took another bite.

Alex shook his head and kept eating.

"I guess it must be an acquired taste." AJ shook her head and dug into her eggs.

Leslie went for her bacon first, savoring the crispy texture while looking out over the river. Then she drank down the strong morning coffee. "Thank you Alex for cooking. I figured I was going to be doing a lot of that on the way, so it's nice to get a break."

He smiled.

Leslie looked out at the camping area and relaxed a little to see Anya furiously packing her gear, and taking it down to the kayak area. Leslie wanted to be on the river as quickly as possible.

Anya stormed over to the fire. "Please tell me there's still food left."

Alex pointed at the pans near the fire. "There's plenty left. Help yourself."

Anya gave a sigh of relief and piled her plate high. "Thank goodness. Yesterday was rough. I can't imagine what today is going to be like. Heading more into the interior, certainly we're going to find more trouble."

Leslie nodded. "We all need to continue to stay vigilant. Hopefully we won't run into any fallen trees like yesterday, but you never know out here. Today though, we should reach the *Toy of the Gods* before the end of the day. Then we can regroup and plan our attack for the hike into the jungle."

Leslie was still tucking away her breakfast when Miguel

pointed at the snake left on her plate. "Are you going to eat that?"

She shook her head and let him spoon them onto his own plate.

Alex noticed. "Not cooked to your liking, eh Miguel?"

They both laughed.

Miguel responded, "I'll say it's passable. By the way, got another jungle story for us? Something that doesn't have gods in it?"

Alex nodded. "Certainly. I can tell you the story of Rabin, the high priestess of the fifty tribes. She was born eighty years ago, and the moment she was born her people knew she was special. It is said that when she was born her skin glowed golden as if a portent that the tribe's future was to be golden." Alex continued, "and so it was that as Rabin grew, the tribe grew stronger. Rabin had her own magic that she used to protect her people.

"She used her magic to help their crops grow, to help their members recover from injury, to help their hunters find game — and she also used her power to persuade. "

"Then one day, the tribe had the outside world to contend with. She decided that in order to protect the jungle and her tribe, she needed other tribes and other ideas to add to her own. So she began persuading and acquiring more tribes and members to join her. She didn't consider herself their leader, but she was. She commanded these tribes and they all grew and became stronger and smarter."

"But, once it was pointed out to her that it was her magic holding the tribes under her control, she became enraged with herself for allowing it. She had never meant to use the magic in such a way and she felt it was a betrayal of her gifts."

"She stepped away from control from the fifty tribes in this jungle who followed her. Now she's but a ghost in the jungle, wandering from city to city."

Anya stood up, having finished off her breakfast. "Don't you have stories that aren't so fantastic?"

"Don't Russian's believe in mythology and magic?" AJ asked.

Anya looked off into the distance, "Yes. We do. But our stories have serious morals." She nodded, "Next time, I vill tell you a story of the Ice Queen, and not that silly ice princess idea that Disney appropriated. The true Ice Queen."

Leslie certainly thought that Anya was a bit of an Ice Queen herself.

"Or maybe a story that doesn't seem so tragic," AJ said as she stood. "Not about a lost love, or a good leader who leaves her flock to roam the jungle alone and lonely."

Alex shrugged. "Some of the greatest stories are tragic."

Leslie wondered if AJ was worried that her story would be tragic. That was to be determined sometime into the future, hopefully long in the future. She poured the last of the coffee into her thermos. Hot weather or not, she still needed a hit of caffeine throughout the day.

The early morning breeze had kept the mosquitos down. Now they were hovering in curtains above the river. Leslie reminded everyone to slather on the bug spray and the sunscreen. The sun was bright, the humidity was high, and the clouds were very much like yesterday— building together in bundles out in the distance.

Leslie pulled her kayak down to the river, then took some quick sips of coffee before climbing in. Out in the water, she thought she spied a small boat in the distance, coming their way.

Alex came up next to her, also seeing the boat and waited with her.

"Shit," Leslie said as soon as she could tell who was in the boat. "Let's get going." She wasn't going to wait for Dan Draper to catch up to them. Maybe by some miracle they could lose him on the river. But by the time everyone in the group had their kayak in the water, he had reached them. He was sweating profusely and breathing hard.

"Leslie!" he yelled, "can you guys take a break! I've been going almost all night to try and find you."

She yelled back, "You take a break. Then head back upstream. You should reach Nauta in two days." No way was she going to stop for the interloper.

"But I have news that you're going to want to hear," he retorted.

Leslie signaled Alex and the group to keep going. Alex started up his engine and the rest of the team heaved on their paddles. She slowed down and angled toward Dan's boat.

This had better be good, she thought.

24

PINK RIVER DOLPHINS

Leslie brought her kayak up next to Dan's boat and grabbed onto the edge of his vessel because she didn't think Dan had the energy to reach out to hers. He was breathing hard. Sweat dripped from his face and curly black hair. He wiped his face down with a bandana and took a drink from his canteen, which she really hoped contained water.

"So what's this big news you wanted to tell me about?" She assumed he had made that up, in order to catch up with them.

"I thought I recognized one of your party. I made a quick call in Nauta and found out they're a felon."

Leslie grimaced at Dan. "Who's a felon?"

Dan shook his head. "No way. It's not that easy. Let me travel with you and tonight, I'll tell you who it is."

Leslie laughed. Now she knew he was just playing her. "No thanks."

"Listen! Listen!" he yelled as she started to push away. "Do you even know who you're traveling with?"

She trusted Miguel and AJ, but it was true that she didn't know anything about Alex or Benignio. But she would rather take on a felon than worry about this man on their tail. "You need to turn around. Certainly no story is worth you dying for."

He laughed and shook his head. "You have no idea."

"Look, if you keep following us I'm not taking any responsibility for you."

"It's okay, lady. I'll do just fine."

Leslie looked ahead, the others were making good time. She'd have to work hard to catch up. "If you make it to our destination tonight, you can join us and tell us all about our felon. But we're not waiting for you. Our goal is the ship, the *Toy of the Gods*. It's on this river somewhere ahead. You can't miss it."

A slow smile grew across his face. He nodded. "Thanks, lady. I'll make it there."

She took her extra canteen, which was an emergency backup, and threw it into his boat. Then she pushed off for some space and started paddling.

It took her about an hour to catch up with the group. It was hard work, but she was glad they hadn't slowed down for her.

AJ signaled her and she approached her kayak.

"What did the journalist want?" AJ asked.

"He says that someone in our midst is a felon."

"Do you believe him?"

"I don't know." Leslie glanced at each of the members of the group, then back at AJ. "When we were back at the resort, did you do any searches on any of them?"

AJ paused paddling and stretched her arms. "How well you know me, and yes, but only on Alex. I didn't have much time since I had to follow up with Samantha on our exit strategy. Not a lot of information on him, just that he's a professor. I definitely didn't see anything about a felony, so I don't think it's him."

"Well, I'm not too worried about it now. If Dan makes it to the boat, we can find out then."

AJ had put her paddle on her lap, but Leslie was having a hard time keeping up with her kayak. It was like AJ's vessel had an engine running. Leslie looked down into the water and saw two pink river dolphins pushing AJ's kayak.

Leslie looked back up at AJ who was still stretching her arms. "Hey AJ."

"Yes?"

"You mentioned frequencies the other day. Does that include talking to dolphins?"

AJ laughed. "I can communicate with dogs and a bird. Other than that, I have no idea. Why?"

"You might want to check your tail end. Also, I'm a little jealous I can't talk to dolphins."

AJ looked back and into the water. Her eyes widened and her mouth fell open; a look that Leslie had never seen on AJ before. If she was going to label it, it would be pure joy. It made Leslie's heart feel a little lighter too.

Leslie pushed a little distance from her. "Well if you're going to cheat, just don't let anyone else see you."

AJ looked at her, a big smile lighting up her face. "I'm not cheating. I was just thinking that my arms were aching and I could use a break. This is nice, but yeah, I probably don't want the rest of them to know." AJ started pumping the paddle into the water, and the dolphins peeled away from the kayak.

Leslie watched the dolphins swim past them and past the other kayaks. One leapt into the air next to Alex's boat and the rest of the team, now aware of their presence, watched them swim ahead and disappear. A beautiful sight that would hopefully keep morale positive.

It wasn't often that they found an animal in the Amazon that wasn't trying to eat them or kill them.

25

A CAIMAN PROBLEM

L eslie's arms were sore from paddling. Up ahead she thought she saw a white dot. She just hoped it wasn't another sandbar. They had already come across three so far, and it took them time to carefully get out, pull their boats over the sandbar, then get started again.

While they were pulling their kayaks over the last one, Anya had stumbled, almost falling into the river. Alex had offered to switch places with her and now he was paddling and she was sitting in his boat, letting Benignio take care of the motor and steering.

The long day was taking its toll. The quick stop for lunch had helped everyone recover some energy, but the heat, sunshine, humidity, and mosquitos were wearing on everyone.

At least a few clouds had rolled in ahead of the coming storm. Leslie adjusted her braid of hair and her hat.

The white dot ahead was starting to get bigger. Leslie thought she could see the outline of a ship, but she could also now make out a tan line of sand in the river between them and what was hopefully the *Toy of The Gods*.

Benignio had turned off the engine and was standing up at the front of his boat, also looking ahead. He pointed and yelled. "Sandbar!"

Damn it, Leslie thought.

He remained standing and staring out in the distance, so Leslie glided closer to him.

"Benignio? What else?"

He looked over, worry etched on his face. "I think I see dark shapes in the water. It could be a caiman resting place."

"Damn it," she said out loud. More than likely the caiman wouldn't bother them, or maybe only nudge the kayaks, but if the caiman were curious or aggressive, the inflatables wouldn't stand a chance against an attack. Plus they'd have to cross the sandbar on foot, leaving all of them exposed.

Leslie turned her kayak to the shore, expecting that everyone would follow her. They'd have to drag the equipment along the shoreline and then reenter the water on the other side of the sandbar. As she approached the shoreline, she noticed rows of dark shapes. The caiman weren't just on the sandbar, they were on the shoreline for as far as she could see.

And up ahead, less of a dot and more of a beacon of hope, was Toy of the Gods. It meant that for tonight they would have comfy beds, a kitchen, and a place to regroup where snakes and caiman weren't trying to kill them. But, they had to make it there first.

She turned her kayak around to the rest of the team. AJ was fairly close. She called out, "AJ, what do you think? Should we try to go around them or through them?"

AJ shrugged and turned toward the sandbar. "Let me see if I can talk to them first. Maybe I can shoo them away." AJ pulled ahead of the group, her silhouette framed by sand, river, and dark menacing shapes.

Leslie held her breath while AJ floated closer toward a caiman sunning itself, so far it wasn't moving.

AJ looked back and shook her head at Leslie.

It didn't appear that AJ had the power to make them go away. How the heck were they going to do this?

AJ turned back to the caiman. Suddenly, AJ pulled hard on her paddles, let out a whoop, and headed straight for her target. The caiman took off just before she hit the sand. It dashed to the side, running over two other caiman in its way and then snapping at a third. Other caiman still lazed along the sand, not caring about the almost battery of their scaly family member.

AJ nimbly jumped out of her kayak, and onto the sandbar, pulled her kayak across, and jumped back into it her kayak.

Leslie was surprised and impressed at AJ's quick moves. Especially after seeing her just last year being out of shape and inexperienced with a jungle environment.

AJ was sitting in her kayak, on the other side, waiting for everyone and looking back as if to say, you can do it to.

Miguel and Alex went for the sandbar next, each unseating a caiman from its nesting spot, then rushing across the sand with their kayaks.

Leslie waited. She wasn't worried about Benignio, but Anya might have a problem getting across.

Benignio didn't look very keen on approaching the caiman, but at the last minute, he turned on the engine and gunned it. Two caiman parted ways to escape the oncoming boat.

Benignio leapt out and grabbed the boat, signaling Anya to hurry and do the same. Leslie beached her kayak next to the boat and all three began pulling it across the sandbar.

Anya couldn't keep up with Benignio and Leslie. She fell face first into the sand and two caiman walked quickly towards her prone form.

Gasping, Leslie let go of the boat, and ran to Anya.

Anya sat up and screamed into the air, a primal scream that stopped the caiman in their tracks. She stood up, then reached into the boat, and grabbed a machete, held it high in the air, then used it to cleave off the snout of the closest caiman.

Leslie and the second caiman seemed to think better of approaching and backed away.

Anya, with another exasperated yell, pushed the boat the rest of the way into the water from behind. She jumped in, and let out a string of Russian words that Leslie was sure were not found in any travel guide.

Leslie pushed her kayak to the other side of the sandbar.

"Leslie, look out!" Alex called.

She turned to find a caiman walking up the sand toward her. She jumped back in response, tripping butt first into her kayak so she pushed off the sand with her feet and pulled her knees up. Her feet on top of the kayak as the caiman opened it's mouth, just missing her boot.

The caiman stood at the end of the sand, watching her drift into the river. She hoped it wouldn't follow.

"Need some help?" Alex asked, floating next to her.

She laughed. "I have no idea how I'm getting into the kayak from this."

He shook his head. "I'll pull your kayak. We've got about less than a mile to go anyway. You stay there and relax."

"Thanks Alex."

He hooked a rope between his kayak and hers and started rowing.

Leslie took a deep breath. There were very few times that she ever had a chance to take a break on a journey. She watched the caiman sandbar slowly shrink into the distance, her caiman nemesis staying on the shore. She watched birds fly overhead, and spied the thunderstorm that would probably be heading their direction that night.

Now she had time to reflect on the possible felon. Was there really one in their midst? Alex, Beningio, and Anya were very much unknowns. Even so, a person who committed a felony might not necessarily be dangerous to the team.

She watched the caiman re-establish themselves on the sandbar. Beyond the sandbar she didn't see any boat following them. Troublemaker or not, she hoped that Dan was ok, that he had turned around and went back to Nauta.

Dan's plight made her think of the stories she had heard of the first conquistadors who had made the journey down the Amazon River. They should have made the choice to turn back, but they had kept going and almost starved to death, all the while torturing and killing natives for their food and information on gold.

So many people thought history had a thirst for gold. Maybe that's why Dan was interested in this journey, maybe that was why they had a felon in their midst. But everyone else was here for other reasons. At least, she thought so.

Tomorrow would be a hard walk into the jungle, and they would probably have several hard days in the jungle after that and who knew what they would come across on their way. She just hoped that everyone would make it out okay and that they didn't have any treasure hunters on their team.

26

A HARD LINE

Rabin pulled her paddle hard through the water to bring her boat up on the sandbar. She was going to catch up to Alex and his group. They were easy enough to follow. Their campsite right by the river had been easy to spot, and even now she could see the paths they had made over this first sandbar.

She pulled her boat over the sand, walking carefully. The poultice she had put on her injury was working, she'd soon have full use of the leg. In the meantime, she hobbled a little, trying to keep weight off of it.

A bird flew overhead, a tunci, its bright orange and blue colors adding to the great beauty of the river. It called to her and landed on a dead chonta palm tree along the river. It called again then took off.

Her stomach gurgled and she nodded. She had stopped at Alex's campsite long enough to cook some of the tiger, but she needed more sustenance, and a dead palm would provide exactly that. She made sure the boat was beached and walked up the sandbar to the tree.

The smell of rot in the air told her she had found a large batch of beetle grubs. She felt along the outside, finding the place that was the softest, then hacked away with her machete until she reached the nest of grubs. She scooped them into a bag and tied the top to keep them inside, popping a few in her mouth while she walked back to the boat. The perfect snack to keep her moving on the river.

As she got back into her boat she thought back to the time she had lived with Alex. If she had been a stronger woman, could she have convinced him to change his course? Would he have stayed with her? But then, had it been her influence that had changed him in the first place?

He had lived a long time, yet it was only in the last thirty years that he had decided to change the course of the world and to find the staff of Viracocha, the staff of his father.

When he had finally confided the truth to her, she had wanted to know everything. Did he feel pain? Did he have magical powers? And when he told her he was immortal she had felt the greatest sadness for him. How many people had he known in his life that were now gone?

Then the question that she was afraid to ask. "Why would you want to rule this world of such impermanent beings?"

He had nodded. "We are all made for something. It's obvious that you were made to rule the tribes and take them into prosperity. There must be a reason I've lived for so long, learned so much about war. It makes sense to me that I'm meant to rule this world, and take them into prosperity. Same thing that you do, only on a much larger scale."

"Peacefully?" she asked, feeling hopeful.

He shrugged. "Not in the beginning. Those in positions of power will push back and deny the inevitable. Money, leverage, and magic, that's all I need to make it work."

She shook that memory away. She needed to focus on stopping his mad quest.

Maybe it was actually resentment that had driven him? His father had never bestowed anything on his human son other than what had come to him naturally from being born when Viracocha and his wife had taken human form.

Back in Nauta, she had sensed Viracocha's energy, although changed somehow. Perhaps he had bestowed it on his son? Gods she hoped not. If he had his father's powers, the powers he had been born with, and the staff, he would be unstoppable.

She closed her eyes and breathed in the energies around her, feeding her soul and body so she could keep going. When she opened her eyes again, she felt renewed. She picked up the paddle and focused on the river in front of her and mission to destroy Alex and all those who followed him.

27

TOY OF THE GODS

A lex pulled Leslie's canoe up to the shore, and she leapt out onto the sand.

"I appreciate it Alex."

He gave her a slight bow.

Her heart felt light as she looked over the grey and white facade of the ship. It was parked in deep waters and here the river ran fast. The sides of the ship were too steep for anyone to climb.

"How are we getting in there?" asked Anya.

Leslie was already digging into her bag. "Easy." She found the key fob and pushed on the unlock button. The gangplank opened up with a hissing sound and lowered onto the sand. "John sent this to me, just in case I had to come after him. Now, the plan is, we tuck our canoes away out here on the shore just in case we need them. Everything else gets loaded inside the ship. Also, I highly suggest laying out your tents and sleeping bags on the upper deck while we still have sunshine. Most of it was wet this morning when we packed up. Tents will rot if we don't get dry and we'll be out in the jungle for days maybe weeks so this is the only time we'll have this opportunity. Also, pick a cabin for yourself for the night. I'll get dinner started shortly."

Everyone worked on getting their gear off of the canoes and loading it into the ship.

Leslie looked out over the river. There were still no boats coming down the river behind them. Dan was nowhere to be seen. If he was still following them, she figured he'd be about five or more hours more. He'd better arrive before bed because she wasn't going to ask anyone to do guard duty tonight.

She unloaded her gear and went to find a cabin to call her own.

LESLIE COMBED through the items in the refrigerator. The fruits and vegetables were getting old. She did find some hamburger in the freezer but thought that would do well for their return to the ship. Instead, she pulled out cans from the cabinet.

"What masterpiece are we having tonight?" Alex asked from the door of the galley.

"Well, it looks like it's going to be beef stew."

"Oh. Any flour and baking ingredients? I could whip up some biscuits."

"Wow, that would be amazing. I think we have everything you'd need."

Alex gathered his ingredients from the cabinet and the refrigerator while she got out one of the big pots and emptied several cans into it.

"Benignio went to visit the local tribe here and see if they have any fruit he could trade for."

"Is that safe?" Leslie had met friendly tribes in the Amazon, but she had also heard of more aggressive tribes.

Alex nodded and started mixing everything into a bowl. "He knows quite a few of the members here. They come to Nauta occasionally to trade for things they need. They also have a large farm where they grow medicinal herbs, fruit, yuca, and maize."

She guessed it would be a win if he came back with fresh produce— and not as a pincushion full of poisoned darts.

Alex finished mixing the biscuits and started forming them. Leslie was stirring the soup in the pot, feeling a bit lazy compared to Alex, but also happy that she didn't have to do any real work for dinner.

Leslie watched him form the biscuits, his hands moving at top speed. "Do you teach cooking?"

He laughed. "No, that's a hobby. I teach Latin American Studies, Archeology, Politics of the World, and a few others." Alex answered.

"Politics, that can be tricky."

"Not really. I'm known for being outspoken but I also stick with the facts."

"Outspoken?" Now she was curious.

He nodded. "I support the idea that dictatorships are the best possible political system."

"What? How do you support this theory?"

"That's easy. You can't look at most of South or Central America without connecting the dots to dictators. The Inca civilization was a dictatorship and they thrived up until contact with Spain."

"Or look at the benevolent dictatorship of Josip Tito of Yugoslavia. The country's economy underwent prosperity during his time and he maintained peace amongst the nations of Yugoslavia."

Leslie's shook her head, glad that she had knowledge on the subject. "Dictators bring prosperity on the backs of others, not really a system I admire. And even if he did bring prosperity, once that dictator dies it leaves a vacuum of power left open for the next power hungry person to come along. The next dictator could be someone like Rafael Trujillo who ruled over the Dominican Republic for seventy years, known as Latin America's cruelest dictator."

Alex waived his flour covered hands in the air. "Say what you will of Trujillo, but he was responsible for banning the slash and burn method of clearing land for agriculture. Exactly the kind of heavy hand we need in the Amazon to keep people from destroying it."

"That seems a tiny fraction of a good thing. Not one of the Latin American dictators that exist right now are considered benevolent. Some of those countries are suffering from food shortages because of poor management. Not my idea of a good system."

"Ah," he said as he put the biscuits in the oven, "I concede that those dictatorships are ill conceived, but when you have a benevolent leader in charge, it changes that. Mainly, I'm saying that democracy doesn't work."

Benignio entered the kitchen with a bag over his shoulder. "Hey boss. I brought the fruit and had a good talk with my friends."

"Great."

Benignio tossed the bag onto the counter and a ripe star fruit rolled out of the top. Leslie's mouth watered. "Star fruit? Fresh star fruit. I feel like I must be dreaming."

Benignio nodded. "They have a whole farm of star fruit. I've also got some bananas."

Leslie and Alex served dinner in the observation lounge. Leslie sunk into a comfy chair with soup, biscuit, and a cold beer from the fridge She wasn't sure she would be able to get back up. Benignio brought her some star fruit cut into pieces.

"My hero," she said and bit into the sweet citrusy fruit. She had often looked for them in the states, but they were never ripe and the flavor had always left her wanting. AJ had sat down across from her and was dipping her biscuit into the last of her soup.

"So what's the plan for tomorrow?" AJ asked.

Everyone was there for dinner, so Leslie figured it was a good time to share.

"If anyone left any gear outside on the deck, make sure to bring it in. There's a storm coming. I also looked at the radar and it looks like we'll have rain most if not all of tomorrow."

At the visible looks of dismay Leslie nodded. "Yes, I'm afraid so. So tonight let's get a good rest and I want to head out of here around six AM."

Anya groaned. Miguel nodded and headed out of the lounge. Benignio went for seconds. AJ stretched in her chair and Alex went out to the deck.

Leslie followed him and looked out over the water.

"Not going to bed yet?" He asked.

"No. That reporter said that he was going to try to catch up to us. I thought I'd watch for him. It's not like we have a doorbell on this thing."

They stood quietly looking over the river, the sounds of frogs and other creatures washing over them.

"There." Alex pointed.

Leslie looked but couldn't see anything. "What is it you see?"

"Your reporter. Beyond the last sandbar. At least I don't see any caiman hanging around anymore so he might actually make it."

Leslie couldn't see that far and was amazed anyone could in this darkness. The moon was only a partial glow through the clouds and getting darker as the clouds grew thicker. She glanced over at Alex who was now squinting toward the river, as if seeing even more.

She moved to go. "I'm going to grab one of the kayaks and pull him in. Otherwise I could be waiting all night."

"No. I'll do it," Alex offered and disappeared before Leslie could get a word out.

Well, she thought, he did seem to have more energy than the rest of the group. Besides, with his eyesight he'd have an easier time navigating the river.

In the meantime, she'd go get a plate of food for Dan and pick a room for him. She heard Alex open the gangplank, slip the kayak into the water, and start paddling against the current. When he moved into a sliver of moonlight she could see him, moving with speed toward the target that she still couldn't spot.

She watched for a while longer, until he had gone beyond her sight, then she moved back into the ship.

She picked up some star fruit to put in her own bag, thankful to have Alex and Benignio on this trip with them. They had been a good addition. But would Dan have something to say about that?

28

A PLAN

Rabin slid her boat onto the shore and jumped out and behind it, hoping that Alex hadn't spotted her. She watched as Alex grabbed the boat of the other man and pulled it with him. She hoped the dark man wasn't in danger from Alex, but there was nothing she could do. Alex was too far away for her to shoot him with her gun and she wanted him to lead her to the others anyway.

The other man seemed too weak to do anything but allow Alex to take the rope to his boat and lead him away. She had been following him the last few miles trying to decide if she could safely pass him. Now she could see he was listing in the boat, practically collapsing while Alex used his beyond human strength to pull both man and boat with him and his kayak over the sandbar.

She ran along the shoreline to find a safe place and discovered a tree with a flat crook in a low branch. She climbed up and sat on the branch. No time for her to get comfortable. She leaned back against the trunk and closed her eyes, sending her projection out and over the river.

From there she watched as Alex continued down river. She could see the other man was lying in his boat, possibly exhausted, possibly dead. Alex was leading them to a ship. Her curiosity brought her closer to the monstrosity.

It was like nothing she had ever seen before, but she had heard of it. The whole of the jungle talked about the *Toy of the Gods* and its captain John Holbrook. The magical ship that could float over sandbars, yet was still a ship. She glided over the top of it. She had entered many wooden buildings in her projection state, but would the man-made materials allow her to pass through?

She approached the wall of the boat and felt her heart, back in her body beat faster. As a projection she knew she couldn't breathe, but she took what felt like a deep breath and pushed herself through the wall. She didn't feel any resistance. She was inside.

If Alex had taken the ship from the owner, she wanted to take this time to look it over and figure out if it was vulnerable in any way. She wandered down a long hallway and looked through each door as she came to it.

Each door seemed to have someone inside sleeping on a bed. Through one, she felt an energy calling to her. It was Viracocha's energy again. There was no way Alex could be back in the ship yet. This had to be someone else.

She approached the bed and looked over the person there. It was a woman, with only her face showing above the covers. Her short hair stuck out in places. Her nose was not that of an Amazon tribe member, but she was definitely of native origin. Rabin went closer.

The woman's eyes shot open and Rabin jumped back.

"Is someone there?" the woman called.

This was trouble, someone who could feel her presence.

Not Viracocha, not even Alex had ever been able to feel her projection.

She moved out of the room and into the hallway.

Alex was entering the ship and a woman was there to help him with the dark man. They had him by his arms and were leading him down the hall. So he was alive, just exhausted. The jungle did that to many people new to its energies. Except for her. And Alex and the native woman— they would be stronger here, closer to the origins of their powers.

The native woman stepped out into the hallway and Rabin moved farther away from her, hoping she couldn't see her projection. The woman moved to help the others with the man and they took him into a room.

Rabin slipped into another room, and looked over the sleeping occupant. "Benignio!" she cried out, although no one could hear her. She moved closer. It had been so long since she had seen her son. She knew he had been helping Alex, but seeing him here hurt her to the core.

She could send him nightmares if she wished, but she would never do that to him. She brushed her hand over his forehead and gave him happy dreams from when he was a child, growing up with two seemingly normal parents in the Amazon.

Rabin floated up, through the material of the ship, and out into the night.

She couldn't actually feel anything physical, but she could swear that the rain felt cooling. As she floated up, she noticed someone was on the outside of the ship. It was the woman from the hallway and she was vulnerable. Here was her chance to at least remove one of Alex's followers. She cast a spell and waited, unsure if the woman would take the bait.

The woman followed the bait. That was all she needed to see, the river would do the rest. Rabin sped to her body, always glad to find it where she left it, and rejoined with her corporeal self.

She stood and stretched, looking over the river and watching the rain pelt the surface. She knew there was a tribe nearby and that Alex and his team would have to leave that ship sooner or later. She would go to the tribe for help, try to explain to them the danger that Alex posed, and see if they would join her and help her destroy him before he could reach his target.

Then she could rest this weary body knowing that she had saved the world from evil.

She climbed down and grabbed her things from the boat, then headed into the jungle, toward the tribe and for what she hoped was help.

29

LESLIE'S FALL

L eslie walked out onto the balcony and wrapped a blanket around herself to keep the mosquitos off as well as the drizzle.

She looked down into the river. She could see the white water where it beat against the ship. The sound was a like a waterfall. The moon was barely visible behind the rain clouds moving in.

A mist was forming quickly over the water and getting thicker. By the time she turned to head back in, it was pea soup quality.

She paused at the door when a voice whispered. "Leslie."

It sounded familiar. She turned towards it. "John?" Was he here on the ship? Had he returned?

"Leslie." It came again. Then he was there, his face in the fog. "Help."

She dropped the blanket and rushed forward, running headlong toward him. "John. Thank god." She got disoriented in the fog, miscalculated the space, and hit something at waist height. Her momentum carried over the railing and then she was falling, into the rushing water.

The cold water on her skin was a shock then she remembered her training for rapids. Feet up, butt down. She didn't want to get her feet caught under any rocks or she'd drown. The water was pushing her hard and fast. When she did a whirl through the water, the ship was already looking small and distant.

She had to get out of the water and fast. Her back hit a rock, hard. She gasped, taking in some water, coughing. She was whirled around again to face away from the ship.

She gave up on staying butt down, she had to get to ground. She started swimming toward the shore, pulling with all her strength. A rock hit her on her side and the power of the water flipped her over twice.

She kept swimming toward shore until she finally felt silt and clay under her hands. Her legs were still in deep water, being pulled downstream. She used her hands like claws, shoving them into the earth to slow her movement down the river. The water was pushing at her, trying to losen her grip.

She pulled, one arm at a time until her feet could touch the bottom. Digging her toes into the silt, she walked her feet up under. She collapsed, water lapping at her feet, and a frog, unperturbed by her predicament, burping and beeping a few steps away.

She turned over on her back and quickly regretted it. The pain from the rock hit made her grunt. She turned back onto her stomach, her side hurt from the other rock hits.

"Damn."

Once her breathing returned to normal, she slowly stood, checking over each body part to make sure she was in one piece. She gingerly walked out into a thin layer of water so she could look upriver. The ship wasn't in sight.

"Damn."

"Ouch." She slapped at a horse fly that had bit her. She had no shoes, no bug repellent, no water, no communication, no weapon, and no food. Gods she hated the Amazon.

There was nothing else to do. She had to get back to the ship as quickly as possible. She'd have to go inland and walk. She looked down at her torn and soggy PJs and lamented that they weren't going to survive this trip. She got down on her knees in the mud along the river, and taking big handfuls, slathered it on her face, neck, arms, legs, and feet. Anywhere that those bastard bugs could get, she wanted to make sure she had some protection.

The best she could do about her feet was pretty much nothing. Any leaves she might use would probably fall apart within minutes of trying to wrap them on. Without light to see what she was stepping on, she could find herself stepping on anything from a barb that had fallen off a tree, to a deadly snake, or even worse, a bullet ant.

She could take her time and scrape the ground in front of her or she could move quickly and hope the way was clear. But wasn't it her rashness that had gotten her here in the first place? She was going to have to remember from now on, any time she saw fog to stop and think before running headlong into it.

She grabbed a downed limb lying nearby and started scraping the ground in front of her, hoping to move or discover anything dangerous before she stepped on it. She felt ridiculous, but she also knew she wanted to arrive at the ship alive and not as a victim. Besides, if something did happen to her no one would even know where to find her. Heck, they probably wouldn't even realize she was gone.

After what felt like a couple of hours, she stopped to take a break, stretching her back but stopping as soon as the bruise on her back twinged.

She wanted to see how far she might have come. She walked back to the edge of the river with a glimmer of hope. She could see the ship's lights in the distance and smiled, knowing that she could make it. She knelt down to put more mud on her skin, the drizzle was washing it off, but stopped when she heard the gentle sound of breathing. It was hard to see with what little moonlight was coming through the clouds, but she could now make out distinct dark shapes all around her on the sand.

Leslie felt tears in her eyes as she tried to stay calm. She was surrounded by about twenty sleeping caiman, one of whom was right by her outstretched hand. They kind of sounded like her basset hounds when they slept. Of course, her hounds were never going to grab her by their teeth and drag her into a river for dinner.

She slowly pulled her hand back and turned the way she had come, being careful to move quietly.

She could feel a horse fly on her arm and it found a week spot in her mud armor— it was biting. Leslie bit her lip as she focused, taking careful steps until she thought she was far enough away from the caiman to swat the fly away.

The moon came out from the clouds, and now she could see how lucky she had been. She had walked right down an open area between the sleeping beasts.

She turned towards her destination and continued scraping and stepping. Then she came to an open space, brightly lit by the moon, so she sprinted for as far as she could. When she hit shadow she resumed dragged her stick through the sand, then a step, then dragging, then a step. Whenever the moonlight would coincide with a break in the canopy she ran, then it was back to the slow, methodical process.

Her back was aching with every lift of the tree limb. She was exhausted, and she didn't know how much more of this she could take. How did the locals do it? They walked around as if by magic.

She tossed the limb aside, took a deep breath, and moved forward. So far so good. She took another step and another, stepped over some vines, then over a hill, then under some vines, then through a vast open space next to a huge strangler fig tree.

Now she could see the light of the ship through the trees up ahead. She was so close. She took another step in the dark.

"Ouch. Damn it!"

She peeled a centipede off her foot and tossed it away. It seemed only natural, she thought, since the last time she had been in the Amazon she had been stung by a centipede. The pain was excruciating and she had no medical kit.

That's it, she had had enough. She dashed to the river. "Ouch." Another centipede. She fell over a vine and lay in the sand, the pain in her feet overwhelming.

30

A CHALLENGE

AJ propped the door of the observation door open so she could listen to and smell the light rain in the lounge. She hadn't been able to sleep so she figured a snack might help. She glanced out at the night. It was inky black and nothing much to see with the moon partially hidden behind clouds.

AJ sat in a comfy chair, put her feet up on the coffee table, and sipped at a coke.

"Comfortable?" Anya asked as she walked up the stairs from the cabin level.

"I think so, yes. You couldn't sleep either?"

Anya shook her head and walked to the bar. She pulled out an orange soda from the fridge and came to join AJ. "I'm glad ve finally get to talk alone," Anya said.

"Really?" AJ was surprised. Anya hadn't shown any interest in talking with her before.

"Yes. I must tell you I'm impressed by your and Leslie's strength. Both of you make good and trustworthy travelers."

"Yet, you seemed angry with Leslie the other day."

Anya waived the words away. "Meh. I have red hair and I'm Russian. I have the quick anger that comes vith it. She gets on my nerves sometimes. But now, it's good to be around other strong vomen."

"Well, thank you."

Anya nodded. "I noticed the other day, in the airplane, you have one of those Kindles and the book you were reading. It was self-defense for women."

"Yes. I want to learn some self-defense moves. My life has become a bit more dangerous in the last few months."

Anya shook her head. "You cannot learn self-defense moves from a book. You need to have the muscle memory of throwing someone over your shoulder, or incapacitating someone tvice your size."

AJ had thought of asking Frederick to teach her, but had been unsure of that approach. Certainly he had moves as a DEA agent. But, she thought maybe, as a researching type of person she could read about it. But she also knew Anya was right. "I'm not sure where to start. Any suggestions?"

"Yes, ve vill discuss it over a game of chess."

Anya pulled the chess board over. The table rocked and the chess board was knocked to the floor.

At the same time, AJ was sure she had heard a banging noise outside. "Did you hear that?" she asked.

Anya smiled as she picked up the pieces, setting them on the board for a game. "Vat? The sound of me beating you at chess. I think so."

AJ laughed. "Well, I'm no expert, but I think I can win a game or two."

LESLIE SLOWLY STOOD and looked up at the ship. At least she had made it this far alive.

She grabbed a branch and threw it with all her might at the ship. From her perspective it only made a tiny ping. She hoped that inside it had made more sounds than that, that someone would come and check it out.

She waited, too tired to move, half-heartedly swatting at the mosquitos and flies that kept attacking. Her mud layer was gone but she was too tired to kneel down and cover herself again.

No one was coming. She'd have to figure out another way. She was going to have to talk to John about that doorbell idea.

There was just no way to climb up the ship. The observation lounge was two stories up and the sides were nothing but smooth walls. There was however a tree with limbs that stretched out over the ship.

Leslie felt tears sting her eyes. She was so tired and hungry. But she reminded herself, she had been in worse conditions and had survived. She just needed to get inside, away from the bugs and catch a break.

She walked to the base of the tree, a fig tree. She was lucky, a vine was hanging down in front of it. In the shadows of the moonlight and leaves she saw something slithering away. Tired or not, she had to get out of this jungle and soon.

She gripped the vine and grunting, pulled herself up, her legs walking up the side of the tree. Foot over foot, hand over hand, she focused on not letting go, on not falling to the ground.

She was thankful when she reached the limb and flopped onto it, resting, shaking her arms out from the strain.

She crawled slowly out on the limb, inching toward the ship. The light inside the observation room was on, there was someone inside. She refocused on the sliding out a little further. She was just above the edge of the deck.

She knew it was over though when the limb gave out with a sound like the snap of a whip. She fell straight down, landing on the ship's observation deck, the wind knocked out of her.

"Hello?"

Was she really hearing AJ? She moved her head enough to see that the observation door was open and AJ was standing there.

She croaked, "AJ?"

"Leslie!" AJ ran over. "What the hell?"

Anya appeared next to her. "Ve need to get her inside. The bugs are eating her alive."

The two of them lifted her up on either side, carrying her into the observation room. Once they were inside she collapsed into a chair.

"What the hell happened?" AJ asked. "I thought you were in your room, sleeping away."

Leslie shook her head. "Something weird happened and I ended up falling off the ship."

Anya handed her a glass of water, which she drank down and then noticed that her hands were shaking.

Leslie slowly lifted her feet onto the table. "I need a medical kit. I have about three or so centipede stings on my feet." She hadn't realized until now that they were swollen.

"Right back!" AJ said, rushing from the room.

Anya shook her head. "Ve need to clean you up, Leslie and see if there are any other injuries. How about I get you to your room?"

"That sounds great, but I don't think I can move." And she meant it. Every muscle hurt and her feet were excruciating. Tears formed in her eyes again.

Anya nodded and refilled Leslie's glass. "Keep drinking." Then disappeared down the stairs.

AJ and Anya showed back up at the same time. AJ with the kit and Anya with Alex.

"My gods!" Alex exclaimed. "I'm so sorry. I had no idea that you weren't on board." He scooped her up and carried her down the stairs with ease. As he carried her, she felt a warmth spread through her limbs and by the time they reached her cabin, she felt some energy returning.

"It was my own damn fault." she croaked.

"I doubt that," Alex said, but didn't elaborate.

Alex set her carefully on the bed. He moved to the door then hesitated.

"Go on," Anya said, shooing him out. "AJ and I have her now."

31

THE DELAY

L eslie woke to a light tapping on her door. "Come in." It still came out as a croak.

AJ opened the door. She set a glass of water, a banana, and a cup of coffee next to the bed. Sunlight was streaming in from the porthole.

"Bless you." Leslie struggled to sit up, her back was stiff and sore, as well as the rest of every part of her body. "Yee gods."

"Yeah, that's what I thought. Leslie, you're not going to want to hear this, but we're going to take a break today and head out tomorrow morning. Everyone's exhausted, they could use a break."

Leslie felt like an old lady lifting her coffee cup to her lips slowly. "You don't look exhausted."

AJ shrugged. "I'm pretty sure I'm different. Besides, well, you look like hell."

Leslie would have nodded if she knew it wouldn't hurt. She took a sip of coffee then exhaled. "I know. I just hate the thought that we're taking a break because I'm an idiot."

AJ sat on the corner of the bed and shook her head. "Leslie, you don't just fall off of a ship. What happened last night?"

Leslie rolled her shoulders, trying to see if she could work out the ache. "I was out there and there was this fog, then I thought I heard John's voice. I swear I even saw his face and I was so excited I went running. I assumed he had made it back. I guess the fog disguised where the edge was."

AJ nodded. "When Alex was bringing in Dan last night, I sensed a presence. I'm not sure who, it might be a darkness that I've been sensing. I'm betting it was that presence that sent you over the edge."

Leslie nodded then rolled her neck some more to get the kinks out.

AJ continued, "Actually, I've been wanting to tell you something." She took a deep breath. "Besides the power, I'm also dealing with, I don't know what to call it. You know that saying how power corrupts? There's this sort of egoism that's come with it now. I'm beginning to wonder if all gods feel that way because of the power they have. This feeling of absoluteness. I've been quiet about it because I'm afraid I'm going to show myself to be an ogre, but it's getting harder and harder to fight it."

"Okay, so you have illusions of grandeur. Got it. Any way I can help with that?"

"If you see me acting like a god, slap me."

"Alright, I won't physically slap you, but I'll keep an eye out for you." Leslie thought for a moment. "What about the caiman yesterday?"

AJ shook her head. "I can't seem to talk to them. I can't reach them. I tried reaching out to them to send them away, but that obviously didn't work."

"Any other interesting powers pop up?"

"I have a feeling that the flame is the one power that I directly got from Viracocha. The others have been popping up as I've acclimated the energy to myself."

Leslie took a big bite of banana, she was starving.

AJ continued, "And there's more. There's something we don't know about the hidden city. Something that we should know. I have these dreams, each takes me a little further than the last. There's something hidden in the city that's important. I just don't know what it is, but I'm beginning to figure out where we have to look."

"But how are you doing? Are you okay?"

AJ nodded. "I appreciate you asking. It's definitely a new thing for me to be supernatural, and it's hard for me to think in that term, but as per my moon coach, that's what I am now."

"Moon coach?" Leslie felt her eyebrow raise then realized that was ridiculous. Here her friend could spit fire from her hands, why wouldn't someone have a moon coach?

"That's what she calls herself. She and I have known each other for awhile, so it was nice to have someone who knows me, but who can also kind of help me with these powers."

Leslie nodded, happy that her friend had found some kind of council for her new life.

"When Alex brought in Dan, did he say who the felon is?"

Leslie shook her head. "Nope. You saw him in the hallway, that was how he was when he arrived. He was pretty much dead to the world when he got here." Leslie started to stand, but the pain rippling through her feet made her regroup in the bed.

AJ stood. "I don't think you should be walking around today. I'll go get you some breakfast. I say get some rest. Everyone will be ready to head out tomorrow." She dashed out the door.

Leslie felt tears of frustration sting her eyes again. She just wanted to get moving and here she was holding everything up. No matter what, they'd have to head out tomorrow. She looked out the porthole and could see clouds gathering high in to the sky. It was going to rain. A storm was coming.

32

DASTARDLY DEEDS

L eslie rolled slowly out of bed when her alarm woke her. She did an inventory of her body while she took two pain killers from the med kit. Her feet were sore, but the pain was manageable. Her back and side were still tender and she had beautiful purple bruises to prove it. There were bug bites all over her body.

She glanced out the porthole. It was raining— cats and dogs and cows by the look of it. She ambled into the shower. This luxury was something they wouldn't have for a while and she wanted to feel squeaky clean again, at least until she stepped outside into the hot, humid air. She dried her hair with a hair dryer and braided it around her head.

She dressed quickly, making sure to throw on her necklace. Magic could be anywhere in this jungle and she was going to do what she could to protect herself from it. She only wished she had been wearing it the other night. She was sure it was magic that had made John's face appear and trick her over the edge. Her necklace might have saved her from the pain and agony.

She stepped out into the hallway feeling optimistic. Alex stepped out from his cabin a second later.

"Good morning Alex. I wanted to thank you for bringing Dan in the other night." She reached out and touched his shoulder.

"Good morning, and you're welcome." He took her hand from his shoulder and held it in both of his. She felt a strange sensation of heat flowing through her hand and arm, similar to what she had felt in his arms last night, but then it dissipated.

She stepped back and removed her hand. "I'm going to go check on our reporter."

He nodded and turned, jumping easily from step to step and disappearing up into the observation lounge.

Had Alex just tried some magic on her? Or was it just her own attraction to him that had her arms tingling from his touch?

She figured that maybe Alex bared watching, but then so did everyone on this trip other than AJ and Miguel.

She knocked on Dan's cabin and heard, "Come on in."

She was pleasantly surprised to find that Dan had finished a shower and was dressed and going through his backpack. "Good morning Dan. As per our agreement I've allowed you to stay here, Alex even helped you get to the ship. Who's the felon?"

Dan shook his head and laughed. "Oh, no. I didn't come all this way to just tell you. I want to see everyone's reaction. I'll do it with everyone together."

Leslie rolled her eyes and left quickly. If she stuck around then she was liable to punch him. Instead, she turned to the observation lounge and walked up the stairs. On the bar were overnight oats, the rest of the fruit from the village, and the coffee pot was on. The smell of coffee put a smile on her face and a drink of the caffeine put a smile on her soul.

Alex was eating oats, hunched over a table with Benignio sitting across from him. Leslie tried to ignore their whispers while she drank more coffee and grabbed some food. AJ and Miguel came up the stairs next, and looked out of the big, wide windows to the torrential rain outside with melancholy faces. Then Anya slowly made her way up the stairs and went straight for the coffee. She placed the tracker on the bar. "I brought the tracker. It doesn't appear as if John has moved since the last time ve looked."

Leslie picked it up and walked over to the windows, Miguel followed her. She turned to orient the electronic map with John's trek from the ship, and it ran just the way she had thought. East into the jungle. She had thought that maybe they could have used the pyramids as a stopping point, but from here that would be an extra days journey South. They'd have to make their own shelter tonight.

Leslie didn't like the fact that he hadn't moved, but hoped that he was just recuperating from an injury.

"Do you people know who you're traveling with?" Dan's voice filled the room. He let them stare at his back as he got some coffee and food and then sat on a bar stool, finally turning to look at them all.

What a drama queen, Leslie thought. She handed the tracker to Miguel and went for her coffee again. She figured she'd want something stronger after Dan talked, but for now coffee would have to do.

Dan took a gulp of food then set down his bowl.

"Vat are you talking about?" Anya asked.

"Yes, Dan. You said back on the river that you did some research and found out something about one of us. What dastardly thing did one of us do?" Leslie tried not to sound trite, but that was how the words came out.

He laughed. "Actually, I've been researching you, your

friends, and a couple of these others even before this trip. I've been learning everything I could before coming out here. Even down to that British guy Benedict."

The wind swept the rain up against the windows and made a mournful sound as it whipped against the exterior of the ship. Leslie took a deep breath and counted to ten while she considered shoving the reporter off the ship, maybe over the deck.

"Oh," Leslie finally responded, "was Benedict a felon? Because I think I'm okay with that. He died about five hundred years ago."

Dan pointed at Leslie and shook his head. "Hold on little lady. I'm getting to it. I just want to make sure I have everyone's attention." He took a drink of his coffee. "I'm just trying to get across that it's not just one person in this group that's got a sordid history. Not only is Benignio a felon wanted for targeting loggers by instigating tribal wars against them, but your friend Miguel here, he was once arrested for breaking into a museum. Then his brother just up and mysteriously disappeared last year. And then there's Anya, originally from Russia, who has a history of unusual activity, so much so that one of my friends at the CIA says they keep running tabs on her. In fact, there are no photos of her that I could find. How is that?"

Miguel, Anya, and Benignio all started talking at once. Miguel stopped though, the calmer of the three. Benignio launched himself at Dan, but Alex stepped in to put a stop to it.

"Benignio has been my friend for many years, and I'm not upset by some missing loggers who were probably in the Amazon illegally," Alex said, then looked at Benignio and pointed at a chair. Benignio sat.

Anya took the lull to speak, her accent now very Russian in her anger. "What does that matter? What does any of that matter? I don't like my photos online."

Dan shrugged and pointed at Leslie. "Just thought she

might like to know who she has traveling with her. Maybe Benignio is here to kill all of you for being in the Amazon, maybe Miguel is looking for treasure, and maybe Anya wants to find whatever gold might be out here for her Russian friends."

Leslie had heard enough. "Alright everyone. Get your gear and meet me at the gang plank. We'll get suited up and head out in ten minutes."

Leslie watched everyone walk out, then poured the last of the coffee and drank it down. She imagined her friend Jessup behind the bar drinking back his favorite whiskey and she wondered what he would say to all this?

She imagined that he would laugh and just shake it off. Of course she knew that everyone had their own reasons for coming along, and everyone had a past. Did that make them dangerous?

But she also didn't have time for this. It was worrisome that John hadn't moved since the last time they had looked at the tracker. She'd have to mitigate on the move.

LESLIE OPENED the gangplank and the sweltering air rushed in along with the sound of the pounding rain. She put on her rain gear and rain pants, thankful to have them. Everyone else filed in one after another and gathered in the last dry space they'd have for a while.

If ever there was a time for a rousing speech, Leslie figured this was it.

"This is our chance, our time to find John. I want to thank you all for being here. I know that we aren't the best of friends, but we are a team and we've been working great together. Today, we focus on putting one foot in front of the other, helping each other get through the mud and whatever else we might find, and hopefully save a man's life."

Dan was taking photos of the group with his cell phone then threw it into a plastic bag. She was glad to see he was also ready to deal with the absolute sogginess of the Amazon.

She turned to walk down the plank and found that AJ was already at the bottom, standing in the rain, tall and proud. Leslie could almost picture her with a gold crown. She joined AJ at the bottom, waited for everyone to join them in the rain, and closed the gangplank doors.

Leslie didn't know what they would face in the coming days, but she was sure it wasn't going to be boring.

33

AN ENERGETIC PAIR

A J walked down to the bottom of the gangplank, appreciating Leslie's speech, but she needed to move, to feel like she was doing something. She also had an urge to start walking into the jungle, to lead everyone to the city. But how did she know where it was from here? She wasn't sure if what she felt was memory or if it was just a crazy idea that would get them all lost if they followed her.

Leslie stepped out to join her and out of the corner of her eye she saw Leslie jump. She followed Leslie's eyes to what had startled her. The native was holding a spear and wearing a gold plate on his chest and not much else. Part of her thought it was amazing how the natives were so stealthy, while another part of her was impressed that the man was wearing his best to honor his god.

She shook that thought away. This native didn't know that she held Viracocha's power.

Alex slid past Leslie and approached the native. He led the man away from the group. From his hand movements the native seemed to be excited about something. Miguel moved closer, as did AJ.

She didn't understand the local language, yet the few words she did hear, she thought that she understood them. She walked closer to Miguel and whispered, "Do you understand what he's saying?"

He shook his head. "I can't really hear. They're too far away. Just something about someone named Rabin."

The conversation was short. The native handed Alex a bag then disappeared into the jungle. Alex came back to the group.

"Nothing to worry about," Alex said. "He was following up on some things Benignio had talked to them about. Plus, he dropped off some more fruit." Alex handed the bag to Benignio and he stowed it in his gear.

Leslie nodded. "All right. Miguel, Alex, let's take a look at Anya's tracker and coordinate our direction."

The three of them took compass headings and discussed the process. Alex would take the lead, Leslie would be in the middle, and Miguel would take up the rear. Alex took off and AJ followed behind him.

AJ unstrapped the machete from her thigh and began working with Alex. When he hacked left, she hacked right, making a path big enough for everyone to follow. They hadn't gotten very far when the howler monkeys, high in the trees began their cry.

She thought maybe they were warning the jungle about the group of humans, until she began to feel the ground shake. She felt like she was on a balance ball at the gym and trying to keep herself from tilting too much one direction.

"Tremor," said Alex, as if it was a normal thing to be in the middle of the Amazon and feel the earth move. But it felt far from normal for AJ and she didn't like that they were surrounded by all these monstrous trees. What if the earthquake knocked one down?

She reached down into the earth with her mind to feel the energy of the earthquake, but it was gone and done before she could sense anything.

"Shit!" Dan yelled from the back of the group. "There were a few back in Nauta last week, but so mild you had to be looking at something that was shaking to know it happened."

Alex shook his head. "There's nothing to worry about. The Amazon is no stranger to earthquakes. If there's another one, we just keep calm, watch out for falling branches or trees and if we see something, get down or get out of the way."

Alex nodded toward AJ and she nodded back. She was ready to continue.

They went about their hacking for a while, oblivious to the group behind them until Alex stopped and pointed out to her, "We're on an old Inca road now."

"How do you know? I don't see anything to indicate that?" The trees and vines around them were just as overgrown as any other place in the jungle.

He pointed up. She looked up at the trees. They weren't as tall here as they were in other areas.

"Also, every once in a while I'm seeing some small pieces of stones along our way. When the conquistadors traveled the Amazon, they reported that the Inca had roads so well made that they surpassed anything they had ever seen in Spain. Flat, wide, and very easily travelable. Probably why we're not walking in a ton of mud too. They had some sophisticated rain drainage created for their roads."

AJ smiled. "I'm glad of that. I just wish the roads had lasted longer."

Alex laughed. "Eventually, the jungle reclaims everything."

They went back to hacking at the leaves and roots. She glanced back at the others. Her and Alex were heading up a hill. Benignio was behind her, then Leslie, then Anya and Dan, and at the last, Miguel. Everyone was looking good.

———

LESLIE CALLED OUT, "Hey Alex! We need to stop for a break."

AJ still felt strong and was surprised to look behind and see Leslie looking a bit bedraggled with parts of her hair hanging down, Benignio was breathing heavy, and the rest of the group was not in sight.

Alex hacked his way to a log and made space for everyone to sit.

Leslie collapsed onto the log and looked up at them. "How can you two go at it so hard? After hours of walking over and through vines and trees and hills in this heat, I'm exhausted but you two are hacking away like you're playing racquetball at an air conditioned gym."

Alex shrugged. "We were just in a rhythm. Nothing extraordinary about that."

But AJ realized there was something extraordinary about it. Last year she had been the last person in the pack, dragging herself to stay with the group, every step a fight to keep her feet moving. The heat, the tangles of brush all fighting her.

Right now she felt invigorated. At this rate, she could go all day without needing a break. The fact that even Benignio, someone from the Amazon, looked tired where as she and Alex were fine, meant something was up.

It meant that Alex was more than he appeared. Was he another of the Amazon gods? She reached out to look for energy from him but felt nothing except a blankness. She was relieved. She really liked Alex, and the last thing she wanted was to find some god was inhabiting him, like Viracocha had done to Sun. But if he wasn't a god, what was he?

34

DARK AND DEEP

AJ and Alex removed another layer of vines and leaves and suddenly there were no plants in front of them. It was empty air. And far below them a river raged. It had long ago cut a ravine into the landscape.

AJ looked in both directions. No bridge that she could see, and they'd need one to cross this twenty-foot crevasse.

"Damn," Leslie said from behind them. "Maybe there's a way around it?" she suggested.

Alex shook his head. "From what I can see here, it doesn't look like it. This break exists as far as I can see in either direction."

"Can you see a bridge?"

Both AJ and Alex shook their heads.

"AJ, I'll go this direction if you'll go that direction. Let's see if we find anything."

AJ nodded, although she didn't like being told what to do. She used the machete to make her way, careful to stay away from the edge of the cliff. After a long session of hacking, she glanced out at the ravine and she spotted what Leslie was looking for— although she didn't think she'd like it.

AJ made good time with the return trip. "I found something."

"Something?" Leslie asked.

She nodded. "You're going to have to see it."

Benignio was approaching.

Leslie waved at him. "Benignio, can you have everyone else wait here for now?"

He nodded and sat on the ground, obviously exhausted.

AJ led the way back and then moved out of the way so Leslie could see what she had discovered.

"Oh boy," Leslie responded.

AJ nodded. "Yeah, that's going to be interesting. I hope Alex found something better."

Leslie walked up to the log that lay across the canyon and brushed her hand over the top of it. "At least it's been cut down to be flat. But with the rain, it's going to be a little slick."

"What do you think?" AJ asked, not liking the looks of the wet log. If she had her way, she would send a runner to call on her subjects to come and build a real bridge and cross with dignity. Subjects? Where had that come from? She had no subjects.

Leslie stood. "It's going to have to do. Unless Alex found something."

They headed back to the trail, Anya and Miguel had made it. A few moments later Alex returned and Dan caught up with the group.

"Nothing that way. Any luck?" Alex asked.

Leslie nodded. "I don't think anyone's going to like it, but there's a way across."

AJ led the way to the log bridge.

Anya put her hands up and stepped back when she saw it.

"This is not a way across! It's just some tree that fell over. We can't go this way."

Alex nodded. "I'm sure at one time the Inca had a rope bridge here, but it's long deteriorated in this weather. The locals who make the journey from the interior probably put this here. It's the easiest method for a short bridge, there are no lack of trees." He kicked at the log. "You can see that they dug in the cliff side to set it in place, so it's not going anywhere. It's solid."

"What I can do is take a rope with me across, then everyone else can use it as a way to help everyone with something to hold onto," Leslie said.

Alex nodded. "I can do it. I've crossed many bridges like this in the past."

Leslie pulled out the rope from her bag and tied one end around a tree directly in line with the bridge and then handed it to Alex. "Please be careful."

Alex took the rope and stuffed it into his bag, then spoke to everyone. "The trick is to move forward quickly. If you fall, you end up falling forward onto the log. Something I learned in military school, a long time ago."

He threw the bag on his back and took off across the log without hesitation. He was across in seconds. He tied the other end of the rope on his side, pulling it tight. He yelled across the way, "All set."

Miguel went next, putting his hand out only once on the rope to steady his balance. Leslie motioned to AJ but AJ shook her head. She would go last.

"Anya," Leslie said.

Anya shook her head. "No. No. No. I can't."

Leslie waived toward the trail. "I understand. Head on back to the ship. We'll come back for you when we find John."

AJ could tell that Leslie didn't expect Anya to do that, besides they needed the tracker in Anya's bag.

Anya grunted then stood up straight, her head held higher. "No. I must. I - I can't let John down." She tested the rope, wiggling it side to side and up and down. "This is definitely not up to code."

She stepped away from the bridge, walked in a circle, then approached again. "I cannot let this stop me." She sprinted onto the log and was halfway across when her foot slipped to the side and her other foot followed. She had hold of the rope and was holding on with both hands, screaming.

Leslie dashed out onto the log then sat as she reached Anya, her legs straddling the log. Alex joined her from the other direction. They both grabbed Anya by her backpack straps and pulled her back, her butt landing on the log. Anya's scream tapered off.

"It's okay Anya," Leslie said. "Put your leg over the log and you can crawl to the other side."

Anya's face was stark white. She moved her head as if to look below.

Leslie reached out her hand and lifted Anya's head up. "No. Turn and look at Alex."

Anya did as she was told.

"Good. Now lift that leg over."

She lifted her leg and Alex scooted back a bit, giving her room.

"Now, put your hands on the log and scoot yourself toward Alex."

Anya had a death grip on the rope, she wasn't letting go.

"Anya." Alex reached out toward her and put his hand on her leg. "You see how close we are. You only have two feet to go. You're so close. Just scoot toward me and you're almost there."

Anya released her hold on the rope and scooted toward

Alex. Leslie followed behind her and was glad when they were all across safely.

Anya crawled onto the ground on the other side and kept crawling. Alex called out to her, "You can stop now, Anya."

Anya tossed off her backpack and lay on her back. "I never want to do that again. I don't care about getting back. I vill valk a million miles to get around this ravine before I vill do that again!"

While Anya was yelling on the other side, Benignio dashed across and now Dan was getting set to cross. He glanced down at the river below.

"I don't think that's a good idea to look down." AJ said.

"I know. In fact, it's a terrible idea." He walked onto the log, leaning forward and keeping his feet steady in the middle.

AJ followed suit, keeping her feet steady, and was relieved to step onto the other side. It wouldn't do to show weakness.

35

CAVE OF DOOM

L eslie took one step at a time, watching her feet with not a care as to what was ahead of her, only that she made that next step. She had so little energy left, the heat and sweat and mud were sapping her energy. Her back and bruises were throbbing and her feet were painful. Then she realized that Benignio, who she had been following, was stopped. The rain had also stopped, a nice change from listening to it beating against her hat, but she could still hear it pouring down behind her.

She leaned back and examined their surroundings. They had made their way into a cave about the size of a studio apartment. Not overly big, but big enough to allow them some shelter, to dry off, and get a good night's sleep without wondering if their tent was going to float away.

"I think this is a great place for camp," Alex said. "We've got about one more hour of daylight before this jungle turns dark and we won't have any moon tonight."

"What if we have another earthquake?" Leslie asked.

He shook his head. "This place has obviously stood the test of time. And it's either here or back out in that." He pointed toward the downpour.

Leslie had a flashback of her experiences with caves over the last couple of years. Both good and bad. She figured she'd sleep close to the entrance, just in case.

Anya, Dan, and Miguel weren't anywhere on the trail behind them that they could see, but the obvious trail led straight to the cave. There was no way that they could miss it.

AJ, Alex, Benignio, and Leslie got busy setting up what they could. They all put up their tents on the flat rock floor, Alex prepped a fire ring on the edge of the cave, and put up a tarp angled to aim the smoke up and out. Leslie went out on the trail, looking for firewood. She was glad to see Anya and Miguel coming up the trail when she returned.

"Where's Dan?" Leslie asked.

Miguel pointed back behind them. "He's back there. Said he'd catch up eventually."

Anya, obviously not caring about hiding her accent anymore sounded very Russian as she looked around and said, "Oh, thank God. To get out of this incessant rain is a blessing."

"Well, if you two could go back out and find some more wood for the fire, then that will be it for the night. We'll be able to stay in here, cozy until morning."

Anya dropped her bag on the ground and sat. "I'll do it later. I'm exhausted."

Miguel moved back into the rain. At least Leslie could count on him. She turned to AJ who was standing tall and surveying the area.

"AJ, could you do me a favor and start the fire?"

AJ gave her a look like she was being asked to do something that was beneath her.

"Would you like me to slap you?" Leslie said fiercely.

The question brought all eyes on Leslie, but it also was the mental kick AJ needed. Maybe AJ realized that she was the best person here to get wet firewood started, or maybe she realized she was being a jerk. Anya must have thought that Leslie was angry because suddenly she stood and headed out into the rain, probably to get some wood.

AJ moved toward the fire ring and put together the pile she'd need. Leslie assumed she was mostly pretending since she knew that AJ could start that flame with the flick of a wrist, very handy in this wet weather.

Meanwhile, Leslie pulled together everything for the evening's meal and noticed Alex heading toward the back of the cave. She decided to follow. If it looked like he was going to use the facilities, she'd turn around, but if he was exploring, she didn't want him going alone. If the Inca had ever used this cave, they could have left a booby trap.

Alex's headlamp illuminated a side of the cave where it looked like it continued through a human size opening. He moved toward it, then noticed Leslie not far behind. "I'm making sure we don't have any animals living in here. Wouldn't want to be surprised in the middle of the night."

She followed him in. The tunnel had obviously been carved out by water. It flowed along the floor of cave and wound in a few different directions then leveled out, coming out to another small space like the entrance. This cave floor looked like glass. Alex reached out to touch it and a ripple went across the water that filled the cave. The ripples then sent light reflections from Alex's headlamp in all directions.

Leslie shook her head in amazement. "If it had been a hot and sunny day, this place would have been a great place to come take a swim."

"Perhaps," Alex said as he took a step into the water. It set off more ripples and reflections, but Leslie saw a shadow move. She grabbed Alex's shoulder and he stopped, knowing that something might be amiss. Alex stepped back, removing his booted foot from the water as they watched an albino caiman, completely under the clear water, moving slowly and stealthily toward their location. It surfaced just as silently.

"Wow, that's amazing," Leslie said. The albino tilted it's head, listening.

Alex put his arm up against her and pushed her slowly backwards. He spoke softly, "We should probably leave him to his space."

Leslie backed out and turned, walking quickly the way they had come. "But what would a caiman eat in there?"

"I'm willing to bet that many animals know there's clean, fresh water in here. It's not like he made any sound, and other than a bat, nothing could see in there without a flashlight."

They both exited the tunnel and looked back.

"I think we should name him," Leslie said.

"Him?" Alex asked, a quizzical look on his face.

"The caiman. It looked like he was the only one. He deserves a name. It's not every day you see an albino caiman."

Alex smiled. "And?"

Leslie smiled back. "Doom."

Alex laughed. "So now this is the Cave of Doom?"

They both laughed, a welcome change for the day. At the entrance to the caiman's lair, Alex stacked up a barrier of loose rocks. "I'll take it down in the morning. I doubt he leaves his cave, but this is just to make sure he doesn't surprise any of us in the night."

Leslie went back to prepping dinner. Everyone had gathered at AJ's fire, which was burning bright now and provided huge comfort and difference to the darkness and rain.

Leslie prepped the packaged turkey, stove top stuffing, instant mashed potatoes, and gravy. Not a fancy meal, but she hoped everyone would find it a touch of home— more importantly they'd need the energy. Tomorrow they would hopefully find John, alive or otherwise, and who knew what else they would come across in the jungle?

36

OF GODS

A J turned to Alex at the fire. "Alex, I'd love to hear a story about Viracocha, if you know any."

Alex nodded. "I can do that. First of all, in Viracocha's time, commoners weren't allowed to say his name. They would call him 'the great one' or 'the sun god.' But in this case, I think you're ok saying his name."

AJ laughed. "Thanks. I appreciate it." At the same time, the energy inside her was swirling at the familiar words of his name. She took a deep breath and focused on the taste of the food.

Alex continued, "As a god Viracocha rarely took human form, because it made him more susceptible to human failings and weakened his powers until he was back in his full god form. The story goes that in 1410, his life mate, the goddess Mama Qucha convinced him to take human form so they could experience life and love as humans did.

"While in human form, his wife became pregnant. Not ever having had a child, she wanted to see it through, which meant she had to maintain the human form all the way up to the child being born.

"It was said that Viracocha honored his wife's request and vacated his human body so he could protect her as a god. At that time, she was especially vulnerable because a city of giants was striking out against other cities and killing any humans in their path."

AJ, as well as the rest of the group, were quietly eating while giving rapt attention to Alex's story.

"The giants were making their way toward Viracocha's city. Viracocha gathered the rain clouds and the water from the rivers and sent a massive flood to kill the giants. To save themselves from drowning, the giants turned themselves to stone. They can be found near the great mountain to the east."

He pointed out into the jungle and the whole group looked as if they could see the great stone statues.

"Because of the great flood, he saved not just the nearby cities, but many believed he saved the world. It was considered a rebirth of the world in a way, and a rebuilding."

AJ could swear Benignio was wiping a tear from his eyes, but then it could just be a drop of sweat too.

Alex turned to AJ. "What's interesting is there are other myths that deal with giants who were out to kill humanity. Consider the twin warriors from your own Navajo mythology. They killed the monsters that would have destroyed humanity. Makes you wonder, since some myths are based in fact, maybe those giants really did exist."

AJ shook her head. "They aren't mythology to me and my people, and someone who comes from this native land should also realize that. There may not be evidence that the giants existed, but that's because the evidence hasn't been found yet or perhaps it was destroyed completely. Whatever the reason, the stories of the Twin Warriors teach the Diné about our history."

Alex nodded. "I guess I've been a professor too long. I talk like this to my students because most of them see these stories as just mythology. I do see the reality in the stories of our gods and I'm glad to know that you do too."

Miguel, Anya, and Leslie got up and headed to their tents. AJ figured she should too. Even if she did have energy to spare these days, it had been a long day, the food had filled her up, and the power that had been spinning inside her was quiet now.

She didn't know if she'd dream tonight, but if she did she hoped it was a normal dream of eating tacos at her favorite restaurant or riding her motorcycle back home and not of gods fighting giants.

37

BURNING

L eslie tossed and turned. She was exhausted but couldn't fall asleep, so she finally crawled out of her sleeping bag and went out to the fire. Alex was toasting a marshmallow.

"Want one?" he asked.

Leslie nodded. "Definitely. I'm a sucker for marshmallows. Although I'm surprised that you would pack them."

"Super light. Besides I have a thing for sugar and out here in the jungle you can burn a ton of calories."

Leslie laughed. She never would have imagined that hard-muscled Alex loved marshmallows. She watched him heat up the marshmallow, constantly turning it to warm it up evenly, then let the outside catch fire. He aimed the marshmallow in her direction. She blew out the fire and carefully picked it off the long stick.

"Alex, what happened to the child from your story? The child of Viracocha?"

He shook his head. "There are no further stories about the child. It could be that it died soon after it was born."

"I wonder what kind of life it would have been for the child. Would it have been part human and part god? Or, if it was real, maybe it was just human. But it could never have lived with its parents in their world."

"True. The stories from those times are curious. One thing I hope to find in the city is perhaps some tablets or writings that might lead to more history and stories from their mythology."

They sat quietly for a while, eating marshmallows and listening to the sounds of the jungle, the rain having stopped. Then Alex stood and stared out into the night.

Leslie was about to ask him what it was he saw when Dan walked into the cave. He stopped, as she had done at the change in scenery. He walked over to the fire and sat down. Even in the firelight, Dan looked worse for wear. He had obviously been struggling to catch up to them. He had bits of branch in his curly black hair, sweat was pooled on his face, and as he took off his raincoat she could see that he had patches of mud all over.

"Whoa. What happened, Dan?"

"I wasn't paying attention and slipped on a muddy slope. Took me hours to climb back up to the trail."

Leslie grabbed the covered pot she had kept near the fire and set it in front of him. He looked up and nodded. Then got out his meal kit and dug into the food. When he was done he pulled out his sleeping bag and curled up next to the fire.

Leslie pointed out, "You'll probably want to put up your tent. Otherwise you might find some new friends in your sleeping bag by tomorrow morning."

"Well, if you want to join me, you're always welcome."

Leslie rolled her eyes. She was beginning to think that Dan was all bluster and pretense, because he certainly didn't mean that.

Dan rolled up in his sleeping bag and turned away.

"Thanks for the marshmallows, Alex," Leslie said, getting up to head back to her tent.

Alex gently took her hand. "Thank you for stopping me from walking into that caiman. I appreciate it."

She nodded and smiled while, again, feeling heat travel up her arm. As soon as he let go it dissipated. She was almost sure now— it seemed that Alex was trying to use magic on her, but her necklace was doing its work to stop it.

What was it he was trying to do? Was it benevolent? Was she just imagining it? And if not, what was a college professor doing with powers of magic? She'd ask AJ if she could read anything from him. In the meantime, there wasn't much else she could do. It wasn't like she could tell him to take a hike.

AJ's tent, tucked against the back of the cave was glowing yellow. Leslie wondered if she was reading or if this was something else. She stopped outside AJ's tent and could feel heat as if she was standing in front of a fire.

"AJ!" she whispered loudly, looking back at the fire. Dan and Alex were blocked by the other tents, no eyes could see AJ's tent.

"AJ!" she repeated. There was a sound coming from the tent, a humming.

She couldn't wait, the heat was rising. She unzipped the tent, the zipper hot to the touch. She could see AJ, glowing yellow, her pajama's starting to singe. She grabbed the top of AJ's pajama pants and shook her legs, not touching the glowing skin. The heat in the tent was like an oven.

"AJ!"

AJ sat up and opened her eyes, they too were glowing yellow. She looked at Leslie. "What do you want?" She sounded annoyed and the glow and heat hadn't stopped.

Leslie slapped AJ's closest foot hard hoping that AJ wouldn't turn her into a pile of ash. "You need to wake up. You're about to set fire to your tent."

AJ blinked and Leslie knew she was really awake this time. The glow in her eyes disappeared and it slowly dimmed from her body.

The both of them watched a bit of ash from AJ's pajamas float up to the top of the tent then slowly fall back down. When it landed on the floor, AJ pulled her knees up, rubbing a patch on her pants that had singe marks.

"My god, Leslie, what is happening?"

Leslie shook her head. "I don't think I'm the one to help you with this. We have the satellite phone, do you want to call someone?"

AJ shook her head. "It's late in New Mexico and in New York. I don't want to wake anyone."

"I think your moon coach and whoever is in New Mexico will understand if you tell them what happened. I'll be right back."

Leslie breathed deeply of the cooler air in the cave as she went to her tent for the phone. When she returned AJ was sitting outside her tent.

Leslie turned on the phone and made sure it could access a satellite. Then handed it off to AJ.

AJ dialed and Leslie wondered if she should give her some privacy.

"Darryl, I figure you're probably sleeping. When you get this message, well, we leave the phone off to save battery power, but I'll try again some other time." AJ hung up and dialed again.

After a couple of minutes AJ shook her head and switched off the phone. "My call to Annie went direct to voice mail too."

AJ looked like she was about to cry. Leslie took her hand.

"Hey, don't dispair. Let's talk." It was the only thing she could think to say. "Tell me what you were dreaming about."

AJ took a deep breath. "I was dreaming about that city. Then I was Viracocha, ordering people around."

"How do you know you were Viracocha in your dream?"

"It was his voice coming from me and I felt all powerful, like I could do and be anything."

"How does that make you feel?"

AJ gave her a look.

Leslie put her hands in the air. "Look, I'm not a moon coach. I'm doing the best I can here to help you. In this case there's nothing I can do, but maybe there's some way you can help yourself."

AJ nodded. "Okay. It makes me feel scared. Am I loosing me? Am I becoming Viracocha?"

Leslie shook her head. "I don't think so. If I had to hazard a guess I would say that you're just having some of his memories. Have you tried taking charge of your dreams? I've heard of people focusing their dreams in order to take control."

AJ shook her head, "I guess I could try, but since I've arrived in the Amazon it's like they've taken a life of their own. I think I'll get changed and take over fire duty for the night."

Leslie nodded. "Let me know if you want to talk anymore."

AJ nodded. "Thanks Leslie."

As Leslie lay in her sleeping bag, listening to the sounds of the night creatures echo through the cave, she realized she had forgotten to say anything about Alex, but then, AJ had bigger things to worry about. And would AJ continue to get worse? And if so, what could Leslie do?

She turned over on her side and tried not to worry. Her friend would get control, she was sure of it. Certainly Viracocha wouldn't have given her the power if she couldn't deal with it, right?

38

ALEX QUISPE

lex put more wood on the fire, the cracking flame just barely heard over the sound of the jungle outside the cave. Since he didn't need much sleep he had decided to forgo it tonight. Last night he had slept for just a short time, leaving his guard down, and had felt AJ reach out with her mind. She had touched his own, and he didn't think she had liked what she had found. Luckily, she was too new at this to understand what it was she had found and he was too close to his goal to slip up again.

In the beginning, they had called him the future of the new world. Now, they called him Darkness, and even his army of the magical and powerful called him an evil genius. It didn't make sense to him. He hadn't changed. He had always been angry about being abandoned, about being different. Now he was using all of it as a means to a new end. To create a new world.

He glanced at Leslie's tent and thought about what she had said. He had told the story of Viracocha's child so many times and no one had ever asked after the child, but she had intuited what it must have been like for him. Being from two worlds yet never belonging to either of them. He regretted having to use her, but he couldn't back out of his plans now.

He just had to figure out why his power wasn't working on her. Was it a natural ability or did she have some sort of talisman to ward off the power? He had to figure it out soon because they'd be close to the city within a day and then the wraths would find them. If he had too much of his power, they would silently attack, siphoning off the power, probably killing him, like they had almost done last time. But with AJ having her own power and by infusing Leslie with some of his powers the wraths would be attracted to them like moths— and he'd be free to find the staff of Viracocha.

And what of Rabin? She was out there somewhere, ready to strike. If only the tribe hadn't let her escape. He would prefer she be kept somewhere safe, out of the way.

He walked the perimeter of the cave, thinking about the timing. It would have to be perfect. The wraths had to start attacking Leslie and AJ, drawing power from them so they would be too weak to fight or stop him, and he needed to find the staff. All within hours of each other. He'd have to hope that without the wraths attacking him and his powers, he'd be able to find the staff this time.

Tomorrow he needed to find a way to give Leslie those powers or the whole plan would be off. He glanced at the other tents. Could he use someone else if he couldn't transfer power to Leslie?

He didn't think it would work. It took a special skill, will power, and character to hold power inside oneself, and he didn't think the others could withstand the energy that would be coursing through them. Unlike his own father, he wouldn't put his son in harm's way. Anyone else would probably die before the wraths even started syphoning their life-force. No, Leslie was the answer and he'd find a way to make it work.

He made his way back to the fire and AJ joined him.

"I thought I'd take the next shift," she said.

"I don't feel much like sleeping right now, how about we both take the shift?"

She nodded.

"Marshmallow?"

"No thanks. They're a little too sweet for me."

Too bad. She'd soon find that sugar could be her friend with those powers of hers.

39

ONWARD

Leslie felt renewed. Even with the short sleep, it had been a deep sleep. And with coffee and breakfast done, she was starting to feel her energy returning. AJ and Alex looked just as energetic as when they had boarded the plane two days ago, although it felt like a lifetime had passed. Benignio and Miguel were looking a little worn, Anya looked frazzled and was staring at the fire, and Dan was still encased in his sleeping bag, snoring.

Outside the cave, the sky was a sapphire blue and the sun was just beginning to rise.

Leslie packed up her gear and everyone else followed suit. Alex set aside some of the breakfast near Dan, but no one moved to wake him. When they were done packing, he stirred. When he opened his eyes and saw they were about to leave he leaped up and almost fell over, still in his sleeping bag.

"Shit, why didn't you wake me?"

Leslie shook her head. "We're not responsible for you, remember? But to be honest, I figured you could use the sleep.

Although, Alex did make you some food." She pointed at the plate of food and cup of coffee that was now cold.

Dan peeled the sleeping bag off, threw back the cup of coffee in one gulp. "Thanks Alex," he said with gusto as he grabbed a tortilla from his backpack. He wrapped the eggs and potatoes, eating his makeshift burrito in a few bites.

Suddenly, Leslie was hungry for a real burrito from New Mexico. Next time she'd have to pack some green chile to spice things up.

While Alex, Miguel, and Anya conferred over the map and compass the rest of them broke up the campsite, dashing the leftover firewood into the forest. Leslie was a believer in leave no trace, and even though the jungle would soon cover any vestige of their passing, tossing the firewood would help to reduce that trace even more.

Leslie glanced into the dark entrance of Doom's home and saw nothing lurking. She removed the barrier so it would be free to roam. She sighed as she walked from the solid cave ground into the marsh of the jungle. If only it would stop raining, but by the looks of the soft puffy clouds in the distance, Leslie figured they would be in for more rain by evening.

Miguel raised his machete in the air. "Let's go." And he set off at the front of the line.

Only an hour later he stopped and let Alex take over. He draped a bandana over his forehead and set his hat on top of it.

Leslie thought that was a brilliant idea and rolled her bandana into the front of her hat. At least it would stop some of the sweat dripping off of her forehead into her eyes.

They paused for lunch, sitting in the first open space they had found all day, a raised bar of dirt that offered a respite from the mud. When they heard thunder in the distance, AJ got up, picked up the machete, and started the line again. Leslie was hoping Dan would have caught up during the break, but he didn't appear.

After what felt like hours, she glanced back. Alex was just behind her but beyond there was no Dan in sight. She slipped in a mire of mud and fell to her knees, cursing herself for not focusing.

Alex called out, "I think we need a break." He came over and helped her out of the mud. "It's kind of you to concern yourself with Dan, especially after you said he wasn't your problem."

"I guess it's a habit, keeping an eye on everyone."

They sat down on a fallen log and took out snacks. Twenty minutes later, Miguel got up and started hacking into the jungle again. One by one, the rest got up and followed him.

Leslie felt she had sweat off about a hundred pounds and most of that sweat felt like it was still clinging to her.

They came to a halt at the edge of a river.

Leslie asked hopefully, "This means we're much closer, right?" Like everyone else, she was exhausted from the hike, the heat, and the humidity.

Miguel drank some water and wiped his face with his sleeve then gave his answer. "If we can make this crossing in good time, I think we should be able to reach the site in a couple of hours."

Either way, the idea that they would soon be at the tracker's location for John was good news to Leslie, and she could tell that AJ looked relieved, as well. Miguel and Alex took some time scouting for the best location for them to cross. Thunder pealed through the sky and everyone got out their rain gear.

Miguel and Alex came back and had seemed to come up with an agreement.

Miguel pointed. "There looks like a decent spot down there. But, we're still going to get wet. Probably up to our knees at least. There's a good sandbar but it doesn't start until the middle of the river. We'll be a little exposed, so we'll have to make quick work of the crossing."

"Let's hurry this up before it starts to rain. This sky is going to open up," AJ said.

They all turned when they heard Dan yelling from the jungle. He was running and pointing behind him, his words unintelligible. Leslie steeled herself for whatever it could be that had scared the man so badly.

He collapsed into the mud of the trail, his arms keeping him from landing face first. They ran up to him as a group, Alex and Benignio taking his arms and lifting him out of the mud. Dan got to his knees.

The growl of a jaguar brought everyone's eyes to a tree nearby. Leslie could see its tail jerk back and forth.

Miguel took a step toward it and yelled. It sneered and snarled at them, leapt out of the tree, and disappeared into the jungle.

Miguel shook his head. "That was a big jaguar."

Dan nodded, breathing heavily.

Leslie held out her hand to help Dan up. "If you get separated from us again and run across another jaguar, your best bet is to grab a rock, a stick, something and face it. Running from it just makes them more interested in you as prey."

Dan barked a laugh and breathily replied, "I'm never getting separated from any of you ever again."

As AJ had predicted, the rain started. Leslie rolled her eyes. She couldn't wait to get somewhere dry, maybe a sandy beach where she could lay back in the warm sun and someone would bring her a mojito.

Instead, she followed Alex to the edge of the river. He jumped in, ending up waist high, and quickly made it to a sandbar, then across to the other side of the riverbank.

Leslie went next with Miguel right behind her. Leslie watched from the other shore as Anya and then Dan made it across.

AJ made it as far as the top of the sandbar when a six-foot long caiman emerged and blocked her way across. It flicked its tail, almost hitting Dan as he scrambled up to the shore with the help of Miguel.

"Holy shit," Leslie said, not sure how they could help AJ.

AJ backpedaled. The caiman ran forward. Leslie was sure that AJ wasn't going to be able to escape, it was running so fast. Then out of the air, a giant bird swooped down and landed on the neck of the caiman and pecked at its face.

The caiman thrashed back and forth but it couldn't get the bird to move away. The caiman rolled, as it had prey in its mouth, but the bird hopped into the air and hovered, waited until the caiman stopped, then landed and pecked again.

AJ was still stuck. At least the caiman wasn't coming after her right now, but there was no clear way across with the giant animals in their struggle blocking the path, and moving into the water could be dangerous. There were sure to be more caiman waiting, lurking nearby, especially after the blood from the caiman's wounds would seep into the water.

AJ looked uncertain of what to do, but suddenly the caiman was coming at her, scrambling its legs toward her while still trying to break free of the bird. AJ rushed back the way she had come.

She was stuck on the other side of the river and there was nothing they could do. With AJ temporarily out of danger, Leslie stepped back from the river and crossed her arms, thinking through their options. Maybe they would have to kill the caiman. She pulled her knife out of her pack, tossed her pack to the ground and headed toward the monsters on the sandbar.

40

AJS ESCAPE

A wind blew across the river, and AJ gasped as she realized the wind was sharing information with her and that information was that Leslie was planning on attacking the caiman. AJ could see the knife in Leslie's hand and she was walking toward the beast.

Then, Alex ran past Leslie onto the sandbar, a knife in his hand. He rushed up behind the caiman, raised the knife with both hands and brought it down in a decisive thrust. He jumped back as the animal rolled, thrashing into the water with Alex's knife stuck in its forehead. It rolled back and whipped its tail toward Alex who jumped farther away.

AJ didn't like that someone or something was going to die unless she acted. She dashed back into the jungle, following the path they had come. She raised her arms in the air and called out to the bird, which looked like the same one that had come to her outside the town. It flew low and hovered above her. She gently clasped the bird's talons and took a deep breath, hoping this would work.

Rain water flew onto AJ in rhythm with the strong beating

of the bird's wings. With three wing beats AJ's feet were off the ground. In four more they were high above the majestic trees, moving down river. Then the bird shifted its wings in a turn and they were moving across the river.

Through the rain, AJ could see the group off to her right. They seemed so small. Their focus was still on the caiman, they weren't looking up.

AJ marveled at the scene around her. High above the trees she felt on top of the world and she realized that she had gotten her wish, to experience the Amazon on the wing. Her heart jumped when the bird swooped downward and again when it swooped upward, but she had to trust that the bird would land her safely.

They moved down toward a small clearing and were quickly below tree level. The bird stalled in mid-air, slow enough to land AJ on her feet. AJ let go and the bird landed and turned to face her.

It bent its head as if kneeling, and she touched a wing, giving it some of her energy, in case it needed it. The bird called out, leapt into the air, and by the time the echo had died it had disappeared beyond the trees.

She ran along the edge of the river in the direction of her friends. As soon as she saw them, she called out, "I'm here!"

The group turned. Leslie's eyebrows shot up. "How?"

"I found another way to cross." She glanced out at the river. The caiman was bright eyed, unperturbed by a small patch of blood dripping down the side of its face, and watching them from the sandbar, Alex's knife no longer pointing out of its head.

"Thank goodness," Leslie said, pointing into the jungle. "Let's move into the jungle then take a break. Get somewhere safe from the caiman."

"Safe?" Anya had stood transfixed by the massive animal

fight. Now she was staring at the caiman, her eyes wide, her hands on her chest. "There's novere safe here." Each word was getting louder, her Russian accent stronger. "There are snakes, centipedes, giant birds, mud, rain, spiders, and these," she pointed at the caiman, "alligators." She slapped at her neck. "And these incessant mosquitos!" she screamed.

Uh oh, AJ thought, she's having a meltdown.

Dan, who had been sitting on the ground, writing notes furiously, got up. He walked up to Anya and yelled at her, "Listen you spoiled Russian." He handed her a tube. "Put on some bug repellent and let's get going. We can't stay here and it's not like we can call up a helicopter to come get you."

Anya took the tube but muttered, "I'm not spoiled." She put on the lotion and handed the tube back to Dan, hoisted her pack onto her back, came up to Leslie and took the machete from her hand, then turned and started hacking into the jungle, making trail for the first time since they had started this trip.

When Anya had moved deeper into the jungle, Leslie turned to Dan. "Thank you. I wasn't quite sure how I was going to handle that."

He nodded, wiping his face with a handkerchief. "Well, I've seen female hysteria enough to know how to deal with it."

Leslie rolled her eyes.

"You send women into hysterics a lot?" AJ asked.

Benignio laughed, the first time AJ had heard laughter from him. It was deep and resounding and made her smile. It had felt like a long time coming.

They followed Anya's path until she finally gave up and handed the machete to AJ. AJ took it and started a steady rhythm of cutting. She could feel that they were getting closer, closer to her friend John and closer to the mysterious city.

41

THE PIT

Leslie gratefully sat down on a log when Alex called a halt to their steady march forward. She took a long drink of water, glad that the rains had stopped and that she saw blue sky above them, although growing darker as the sun was beginning to dip beneath the tree tops.

Alex, Miguel, and Anya took a few minutes to hover over the locator. Alex nodded and waived everyone toward him with his machete in one hand and the locator in the other. "We're close everyone. Follow me."

That was all she needed to hear to get back up.

Alex took the lead, hacking at the jungle with fervor. So fast that it was hard to keep up with him.

After fifteen minutes she began to wonder if they were really that close. Everyone had fallen back and Leslie was doing her best to get through the mud and vines. After a short while the mud cleared up and the trail was easier going.

As Leslie approached Alex she could see he was on his knees, looking down at the ground. Then she could see the large dark hole. "This is where the locator is showing John's location."

It was a pit filled with sharp wooden poles at various heights, and a layer of water from the recent rains. She knelt down next to Alex.

He pointed at the various pikes. "This was more than likely an ancient pit, where the Inca would toss their enemies in if they weren't important enough to be sacrificed to the gods. You can tell someone remade these not too long ago. Maybe about fifty years. Otherwise, these pikes would have fallen apart."

Leslie nervously looked for signs of John on the floor of the pit but it was too dark to see clearly. She pulled out her flashlight from her pack and shone it around. She was shocked to see several emaciated skeletons. Certainly bodies would have long been decimated by time, but then these pikes were more recent. She spotted a boot, but no body to go with it.

Alex pointed across to the other side. "Looks like someone figured a way out."

She pointed her flashlight that way. There was a makeshift ladder leaning against the wall of the pit. It had been fashioned from the pikes in the pit, having been sawed into smaller sections and held together with what looked like bands of leather.

Alex continued, "Smart. Someone survived and made it out. I hope that was your friend John."

Leslie went to the ladder and climbed down. Alex kept his flashlight on her as AJ and the others began to arrive.

"Be careful down there," AJ said.

Leslie stepped in a thin layer of water and made her way over to the boot. It was attached to a short section of pike. The pike had entered the boot through the outside edge, and more than likely would have punctured the individual through the side of the foot. Someone had sawed the pike off above the boot, more than likely to pull their foot off.

The laces were missing, probably what had been used to secure the ladder. She picked up the boot. Glad to see that it was empty of any human remains, although the edges of the hole in the boot were bloody. She turned the boot over and the sole of the boot was already coming off, inside was the locator that Anya had placed there.

Leslie looked up at Anya. "I don't supposed you put another locator on him?"

"Damn it," Anya said and shook her head. "Leave it to that infuriating man to loose the one boot that ve need to find him."

Colorful items in the mud drew Leslie's attention. It was a small circuit board, under that, plastic pieces of a satellite phone. He must have landed on it when he fell.

She also spotted a pile of firewood. He must have had to take his time getting out, making a fire as best he could to cook while he found the energy to build the ladder.

Leslie took the boot with her, climbed out of the pit, and tucked it into her bag. She looked around them at the jungle and tried not to let tears form in her eyes. They would find John. They had to. They only had about two more days' worth of supplies, so it had to be soon.

42

LOST LOVE

Alex was relieved that the pit was empty. If they had found John, they'd have had to stay close by for the night. It would have been too dark to move on and they would have headed back to the ship in the morning. He needed more time to find his way into the ancient city, and he needed AJ and Leslie to be nearby in order to be bait for the wraths.

Tonight he'd give those temporary powers to Leslie. He had noticed her necklace, carnelian red stones and copper. It was possible it was a talisman and had warded off his attempts at the spell to infuse her with power. He'd have to figure out a way to get it off her and try again. If he had to use his powers of persuasion to seduce her, then that would be an added bonus.

He nodded in the direction they had been going. "Let's find a space for camping."

"I know we need to stop, but I hate to when we're so close." Leslie lamented.

Alex nodded. "I know. Your friend is probably close by, but

he's probably setting up camp too. It's getting dark and soon it'll be pitch black."

Leslie nodded and sighed.

He found a clearing under a strangler fig and set up his tent not far from Leslie's, just in case. Then went to work gathering wood for the fire.

From the jungle he paused and watched AJ as she lit the fire. She pretended she was lighting a match, but he knew that she was using her power. There was so much more she was capable of and there she was starting campfires. He realized his fists were clenched. He took a breath and released them. Perhaps, if she survived the next hurdle, he could convince her to join his army. He didn't think she would, but to have that power at his service would be fitting— and the universe owed him.

When he got back to the fire with a stack of wood, Leslie was making dinner. "Smells like lasagna," he said, taking a deep breath and his stomach answering with a hungry groan.

She nodded. "It's pan lasagna. I even brought some vacuum sealed parmesan cheese."

Alex smiled. At least he had eaten well on this journey.

As Leslie bent down to stir the pot at the same time that Alex heard a hummingbird zoom by. Another sound of a hummingbird and something small and dark flew close to Leslie's head.

"Stay down! Someone's shooting darts!" Alex dashed into the dark jungle.

When he made it into the darkness he dropped on all fours and stopped, listening. His ears could pick up more sounds than a human's could. He heard the steady movement of a foot on the jungle floor, and someone breathing in deeply, likely about to deliver a dart. He leapt up in the direction of the dart breather.

The long green leaf was wrapped up into a tube held at mouth height. He slapped it away, knowing it was pointed at his friends at the fire. Angry at the possibility that they could be injured or killed, he backhanded the person and sent them flying.

He heard the familiar voice of Rabin as she screamed and flew backward into a tree. He immediately regretted his move. He ran forward, following the trajectory of the woman as she flew through the air.

He found her lying face down. He carefully turned her over, he had to see her face, those eyes.

"Rabin?"

She opened her eyes. He was hit hard by the overwhelming sadness that radiated from her. He could feel the magic in her too, but it was waning and not just from the hard landing— he could feel she was getting too old, as well.

Alex suddenly felt angry again. "Rabin, I gave you a chance at a real life. A life of greatness."

Rabin started crying and she ran a hand over his face. "I hate that you have this insanity, this drive."

He couldn't stand her crying. He pulled her in closer then heard sounds from the camp, the team was stirring, looking for him.

"Alex, are you ok?" Leslie called out.

Then he realized that he could use this situation to his advantage. He picked up Rabin in his arms and ran, carrying her far into the jungle away from the camp, but close to the city. When he came to a stop, he set Rabin down carefully.

He yanked down a liana from a fig tree and wrapped it around her body, then pulled it up against the tree, wrapping it several times to make sure she wouldn't get free.

"Rabin, I'm sorry that you couldn't follow me on my path. I never wanted any of this."

She reached up with one hand and held his face near hers. "Alex, stop what you're doing. You don't want to do this. It's not right."

He could feel that she was trying to use what little magic she had left on him. She had never had any power over him, not like that anyway.

"I'm doing what's right, Rabin. You saw how your tribes prospered under your command. Benevolence and command are what's needed in this world."

He cast his spell. Rabin was in no shape to protect herself from it. His power infused her. Her eyes grew bright and she turned her head to the right a bit, her way of thinking about a problem.

"What are you up to? Why haven't you taken the staff yet? You certainly wouldn't be back here if you had it already."

"I'm using the people with me to attract the wraths of the jungle so I can reach the staff safely."

Her mouth opened and her eyes widened.

Alex shook his head placing his hand on her shoulder. "Not Benignio. He'll be safe with me."

She let out a sigh. "So they don't know what you're up to."

Alex nodded. He was comforted by the fact that she would die peacefully. The wrath would sap her energy slowly and she would fall asleep before she knew what was happening.

He kissed her on the forehead and turned back toward the camp, running back the way he had come. He wished that Rabin had wanted to change with him. She had been his greatest inspiration.

He could easily be the earth's king. He would have a kingdom greater than his father's ever was. Soon he would have what he needed for the next phase.

He knew the secrets of life and he knew the destruction of

death. He had seen so many lovers die and soon he'd have the power, the power to save those he wanted to keep in his life and the power to destroy. And the power to command, everyone.

NIGHT

AJ wondered if she should follow Alex but he had disappeared so quickly into the jungle. She hesitated when she realized it was beneath her to be running around in the jungle, she should let Alex take care of it. Then she mentally slapped herself. She needed to get a grip on reality. She was not an omnipotent god. She was flesh and blood with just a few tricks up her sleeve.

Leslie had moved one of the pop up tents between her and the direction the dart had come, and resumed huddling over the food. She could see that Benignio, Miguel, and Anya had moved behind some trees, knelling down together, with Benignio watching the direction the dart had come. AJ knelt down next to Leslie.

"Still cooking?"

Leslie pointed at the pot of food. "I didn't pack this stuff in so it would go to waste. Either we get overrun by natives and they force me to stop cooking, or I'm going to keep going."

AJ nodded. She felt a sudden flash of evil from the jungle that jolted her. It was like a dark spirit, someone deeply troubled and angry, had lashed out. The feeling was gone as fast as it had come.

"AJ?" Leslie asked.

AJ shook her head, realizing she was grimacing. Her feelings of godness were gone as well, cowed by the strong evil.

Alex returned, walking confidently. "It's fine. It was a local tribesman, he thought we were poachers. I was able to talk with him."

Leslie bolted up. "Did you ask him about John?"

He nodded. "Sorry, he hasn't seen him."

Leslie sat back down. AJ could feel her disappointment.

Miguel, Anya, Benignio, and Dan came out from their hiding spots and joined them at the fire.

Leslie waved at them, "You should all get your meal kits. Dinner is almost ready."

AJ ENJOYED DINNER, but kept her eyes on the dark jungle. The mood throughout the group was subdued.

She scanned the jungle. The evil wasn't there anymore, but she could feel an excitement in the air, a stirring of things in the jungle. She couldn't pinpoint what it meant, then she felt the ground rise and fall in tiny tremors.

Her friends at the fire looked unconcerned. She realized that with their weak ability to feel sensations, they didn't even feel the movement. She could see the leaves in a nearby tree shake slightly, but they would probably think it was just a wind.

AJ closed her eyes and focused on the tremors. She could feel that the they were coming from the North, the direction of the fault line and the active volcano. The waves in the earth were small and steady, she sensed there was no danger of them getting stronger. She reached out and imagined grasping a wave in her hands, making the wave taller.

"AJ!" Leslie's voice roused her from her focus.

The rest of the group were standing now, most of them with their hands out to keep their balance as the earth tremors passed.

"Are you okay?" Leslie asked her. AJ nodded as the tremors calmed back to the small almost undetectable movements. She smiled at her friend but inside she was worried. She had done it without thought as to what might happen to everyone else, the jungle, the natives.

Miguel shook his head and sat down. "Let's hope we don't have too many of those. Last thing we need are the trees toppling around us."

Benignio spoke in Spanish, long sentences that made no sense to AJ, but she also understood his frustration with all the things the jungle was throwing at them. Little did he know that she was one of those 'things.'

The other night she had almost burned down her tent; today, she had almost set the whole Amazon shaking. Should she leave the group? Would they be safer without her?

Anya sighed, sat back down on the ground and leaned onto Beningio's leg. "Vat's our next step?"

"According to Benignio," Alex pointed at his guide, "the remnants of the old city are near here. The city that I am here to find. I say we go there in the morning. There's probably shelter there, and John might have gone searching for a place out of the rain."

At the mention of rain, the sky in the distance answered with a flicker of lightening. Anya groaned, "Uh. No more rain, please." Then she brought the conversation back to the subject. "Yes. This city. It vas vere John was originally going."

Leslie looked unconvinced. "I don't know. How would he

know if any structures survived after all this time? Why not try to head back to the ship? Or maybe he did and we just missed him. Or perhaps he's turned around and in shock from the injury and has no idea where he's going."

If AJ were injured and alone in the jungle, where would she go? But then, her dreams had been bringing her to this place all along. She realized she couldn't leave without seeing what was left of that ancient city.

Anya shook her head. "No. If you really knew John, you'd know that he vouldn't go back to the ship without finding vat he vas looking for. Injured or not. He's out there looking for that city."

AJ saw the look of anger pass over Leslie's face.

Dan, who had collapsed onto the ground by the fire, shook his head. "Of course, Anya's more interested in the city than in John. You all worried about her yet?"

Anya leapt up, grabbed an empty pot by the fire, and walked toward Dan with the pot in the air. It was the fastest AJ had ever seen Anya move. She muttered a string of Russian words that no one understood, but everyone knew what she meant.

Leslie didn't get up to stop Anya. She did turn to Dan and said, "Do you have any proof that makes Anya shady? If not, then I suggest you lay off the innuendo before Anya puts a dent in that pan."

Dan kept his gaze on Anya, who was poised to lash out, her eyes full of fire. He put his hands up in surrender. "Sorry Anya. Seriously, I'm sure you're a good person." It was insincere, but Anya lowered her arm.

Her Russian accent thick. "You're not vorth it. I'll save my energy for more important things." She dropped the pot, grabbed up her food and moved away from the fire.

That seemed to be a signal. The rest of the group slowly got up and moved to make for bed. Dan pulled out his sleeping bag and got cozy near the fire.

AJ stood. Leslie had enough to deal with right now with this ragtag team, she didn't want Leslie worrying about her. She'd do her best to control herself. Meanwhile, they were so close to the city, she could feel it all the way in her bones and she hated to be going to sleep to only dream of the city. Night or not, she wanted to be in the city for real. She looked out into the darkness and wondered what they'd find there tomorrow.

Maybe tonight, she'd try to control the dreams like Leslie suggested.

44

A WORRIED MIND

Leslie finished putting away everything from dinner. The rest of the group were in their tents and Dan was leaning back against a log at the fire.

Dan nodded towards the tents. "Did you see how fast she moved?"

She knew he was talking about Anya. Normally, Anya walked and moved with the speed any normal person might have in the Amazon. But when she had moved at Dan in anger, it had been at lightning speed. A move Leslie hadn't thought Anya was capable of. Leslie nodded.

Dan continued. "From what I understand she was a spy. Not sure if that's still true, but she's definitely more dangerous than you think she is."

Leslie shook her head. "Actually, I know that everyone here is dangerous. We all have our secrets, desires, goals that may conflict with one another. I just hope that this alliance we've all created lasts until we're safely out of here. As for Anya, I'll keep my eye on her."

Dan nodded and lay back in his sleeping bag. "I'll take a watch tonight."

"Hmmmm. So when I say we're all dangerous, I'm including you."

"I'll tell you a secret little lady."

"Sure, as long as you never call me little lady again," Leslie said.

He laughed. "Fine. Leslie. I once lived here in the jungle."

"What?" Leslie shook her head and looked over at the man who was barely keeping it together,— although he had kept up with everyone since the jaguar and he had taken some time to shake out his gear for once.

He nodded. "Yep. It was about thirty years and many pounds ago. I was a college student and my project was working with a professor on the communication techniques of the Tiquanda tribe. I lived with and got to know them. I cowrote a book about them. The techniques they used to survive the jungle were astounding."

"Used?" She didn't like the way he said it, so final.

He stared out into the distance. "A Christian group, bent on bringing God to the jungle came along. Apparently one of them had the flu. It all but killed most of the tribe and the two that survived moved in with another tribe. The only records of them are in that book I wrote with my professor."

"That is a terrible tragedy, but what are you trying to say?"

"That you don't have to worry about me. I've stopped smoking, and I'm getting my jungle legs back. Look, I know I haven't been the best member of the group. I want to help pull my weight. Besides," he looked sheepish, "I appreciate that you've been feeding me. I know you didn't have to do that."

Leslie nodded, trying to keep the surprise she felt from showing on her face. "Ok. When you feel you've pulled a couple of hours of watch, wake someone else to take over."

"You got it."

Leslie yawned as she walked to her tent. She was tired and worried. About everything. The look she had noticed in AJ's eyes earlier, it was the same look she had seen in Sun's eyes. She felt a sense of deja déjà vu to Sun's outburst that had killed a member of the group. Was AJ on the edge? Was she too close to the home of Viracocha to control the powers? And Dan had simply mentioned what she had been thinking when she saw Anya lash out. Anya was hiding something.

And everyone was insistent on seeing the city. But it wasn't as if she had any other ideas to chase. Unless they ran into some locals who knew where to find John, they were stuck.

"Damn it, John. This is all your fault," she whispered. "Yours and that ancestor of yours who thought it was a good idea to go running around a wild jungle." Although, she also admired Benedict Spafford. He had explored places that were even now considered inhospitable. She slapped at a mosquito buzzing in her tent and wished she could be on a trip in the arctic. A nice simple trip from the old days when she didn't have to worry about stray gods, cities that might contain gold, or people that might go a little loopy for said gold. Then there was Alex, smooth talking, handsome, yet with an undercurrent of power. Was he really here to do research? At least she had one person on the team she trusted. Miguel was a good man.

She used a little of her drinking water to wash up a bit. She took off the necklace to clean the sweat and dirt that had collected underneath, then lay on top of her sleeping bag, listening to the breeze, the wall of sound coming from the animals and bugs in the jungle, and the crackling of the fire until it all lulled her to sleep.

45

ALEX FOLLOWS

Alex stepped out of his tent. He couldn't sleep. The wraths should be here by now, attracted by the power coming from AJ and Rabin. But he couldn't feel them nearby.

Maybe it was possible that he could get Viracocha's staff and leave without the wraths interfering at all, but he'd rather be sure that they wouldn't attack him. If they did, even with the staff he might not be able to make it out of the jungle. He wasn't even sure the staff would work for him. He was, after all, only a half god. He might have to find another way to get the wraths here to go after his decoys and ensure that he stayed safe.

Alex started toward the fire but saw that Dan was up, tossing fuel onto the fire. Alex wasn't in the mood for conversation. He stepped toward the jungle, but knew that Rabin was out there, bound to a tree. He didn't want to see her. She might try to talk him out of his plan.

He stopped when he heard AJ's tent zip open.

AJ stepped out, still dressed in her clothes from the day, her eyes closed. She was walking barefoot, her strides confident.

Alex smiled. If she was dreaming, maybe she was dreaming about his prize. He didn't know where it was in the city, but there was a chance that AJ knew, even if only subconsciously. He used his power to put up a wall of illusion around the two of them, just in time.

Dan stood up from the fire and looked over at the tents, probably curious about the noise from the tent opening. Dan shook his head and sat back down, facing the fire.

Alex looked around to make sure everyone else was still sleeping. Satisfied that they wouldn't be stopped, he followed AJ into the jungle.

He wondered what AJ would think of him if she knew he had been the mastermind behind the skinwalker that she had tangled with in New Mexico? He wanted the chance to talk her into his side of things, so he didn't think he would ever tell her, that is, if she even survived the next few days.

46

AJ'S DREAM

AJ was exhausted from the day. She figured it was just as much from the stress of not finding John than from anything else. Even as she entered her dark tent she could feel the dream calling her, but she was determined to get comfortable and to be aware of her surroundings, if she could. She took off her boots and socks to feel the fresh air on her tired feet.

Sitting on her sleeping bag felt so comfortable. She'd close her eyes for a moment and then finish getting ready for bed. But she entered the dream as if on command.

She was outside the city, near the street. She'd have to walk through the jungle to reach it, but the street was glowing silver in the sunlight, easy to reach. She started walking fast, knowing she wouldn't have long before the dream ended and she'd be back in the real world, wondering more about what she was missing. She needed to see what it was in the middle of the city that was so important, but it would take her awhile to make it there.

She reached the road then turned right toward the city.

There was no one else on the road with her. She climbed a small hill and there were the gates of the city. They were closed this time, but she waved her hands and they parted, as they should for a ruler.

A large stone snake guarded the top of the entrance, its diamond shaped decorations sparkling in the morning sunlight. Beyond the gate was the plaza. The gold covered water fountain graced the center of the plaza. She knew from other dreams that an intricate series of tunnels funneled all the rain to this fountain in order to maintain dry streets and clean the water so it was drinkable.

She approached the fountain and touched it, and felt the warmth of the gold in the sunshine. She turned and walked through the narrow streets, turned into an open doorway, then faced a wide trapezoid shaped door. She waved her hands yet somehow knew that it wouldn't open that easily. She pushed at the door, using the handle, but it didn't budge. She paused to look at her hands, the masculine hands of Viracocha, a strong god for his people.

She filed that away, it wasn't important right now. She pulled on a gold ring that stood out from the side of the door, shaped much like the handle. Still nothing.

But this was important. She needed to get through the door. But standing here wasn't getting her anywhere. She stepped back out onto the street to examine the building from the outside. She'd find a way into that room.

She raised her hands again, they were still masculine, still Viracocha's hands. She remembered using those hands to greet the Spanish when they first arrived, as well as to strangle the life from a Spanish priest who had suggested that he, Viracocha, was not a god.

A voice cut through her thoughts, "AJ, I think you need to wake up."

AJ opened her eyes and turned to the man standing next to her. She didn't recognize him at first, then she realized where she had seen that facial structure and the shape of those eyes long ago. "Lllapa?"

The man's eyes narrowed. "I don't go by that name anymore."

AJ shook her head, what was she even saying? Why would she call Alex by another name? And where was she? "Alex?"

His face softened. "Sorry AJ. I didn't know if it was safe to wake a sleep walker, but I didn't want you to hurt yourself."

She nodded. Alex reached out his hand. "Come on. Let's go back to camp."

He turned on a flashlight and she could see that they were surrounded by short stone walls. She glanced over to where the doorway had been and was surprised to see the building and doorway still standing.

Alex waived the flashlight. "Come on. Let's get some rest. We'll be back here in the morning."

She realized then that she was barefoot, and her feet were on cold, flat stone. In front of them was what was left of the old road. Most of the stones were covered in dirt and new growth, but some of it was still recognizable as a path. She started off with Alex next to her.

"Thanks, Alex. I would have been a bit lost if I had woken up here by myself."

"You're welcome. Sorry I let you walk so far though. I didn't want to wake you while sleep walking. I'm not sure if that's a bad thing or not."

AJ wasn't sure either.

They walked in silence for a while, although the creatures of the jungle spoke loudly along the way.

"Stop!" Alex called and put his hand up to punctuate the concern in his voice.

AJ stopped where she was, followed Alex's eyes, and watched a foot long centipede cross their path. She didn't want to imagine what that would have felt like to step on.

"The camp is not much farther," he said.

In just a few more feet she could see the campfire. They reached the turn off from the stone path. Alex turned to her. "Look, this might not be the most comfortable thing, but I can throw you over my shoulder and carry you the rest of the way."

AJ looked across the space of vines and dirt and leaves. They wouldn't be able to see if anything was underneath. She nodded. "Ok."

He had been right. His shoulder dug into her stomach but at least she was not going to get stung. No one at the fire said anything. She realized Dan was snoring in his sleeping bag and there was no one on watch.

Alex seemed to catch her thoughts. "I'll go on watch for a while. Seems Dan has lost interest." He dropped her off at her tent.

She thought it strange that he waited as she slipped into her tent, but she realized he was just concerned. She sat and turned to face him.

"Sleep well." He touched her on her forehead.

The name Lllapa, the Inca word for thunder came to her mind as she slipped away into sleep.

ELECTRIC BLUE

L eslie woke at the sound of movement outside. There was a blue light, a filter on someone's flashlight maybe? She unzipped her tent to see that Alex was sitting cross legged, his back to her, not far from her tent, and he was glowing blue.

What the heck? She crawled out of her sleeping bag, slipped on her boots, and crawled out of her tent. She thought she might sneak up on him but then realized that more than likely he had set himself up outside her tent on purpose.

She didn't feel fear, but maybe she should. "What's going on Alex?"

He turned toward her, his eyes glowing bright blue. He stood up and stepped closer. Leslie could feel the heat from his body. She wasn't sure if it was from the glow, or the fact she had to admit that she was attracted to him. He stepped even closer.

She put her hand up between them. "Why don't you tell me why you're glowing blue before you get any closer."

He put his hands together and opened them to reveal a blue

rose. He tossed it to her and she caught it without thinking. It disappeared and her hand was enveloped in blue light.

"What is happening here?" she asked. Leslie's breath caught as a warm sensation spread from her hand to the rest of her body.

Alex reached out and placed his hand in front of hers, a blue streak of electricity running from his hand to hers. "Power transfer. How does it feel?"

Leslie tingled but she didn't want to tell him that. "I feel fine." She took a step back but it didn't stop the stream. "Why are you doing this?"

"I want you to feel what it's like, to be me." He stepped closer and took her hand in his.

Certainly this couldn't be safe, being infused with blue electricity, but she found herself being drawn to Alex. She let him take her other hand. Then he pulled her close and wrapped his arms around her. She ran her hands up his arms, the muscles felt like a statue of steel.

He pulled her in for a kiss. The second his lips touched hers she felt her body melt. His lips were warm and she could feel the passion in the kiss.

She opened her lips to him without meaning to, she could feel heat flowing into her.

She pushed back and he let go. She would have fallen backwards, but he caught her arm and steadied her. Her whole body was on fire.

His face looked determined, yet somehow concerned. "I have a plan and I have to see it through. Someday, you'll understand." He looked as if he might say more, but then shook his head. He stepped toward her and placed his hands on her shoulders, turning her around and heading her toward her tent.

"Who are you?" She asked him.

"My father called me Lllapa. My mother named me Alex. It means savior of the earth. She thought I'd make this world better, then she left me behind with humans."

He touched her forehead and her body went weak, he lowered her onto her sleeping bag. "Just remember, when you wake up...."

She could barely hear the rest of the words, whispered in her ear. But it all made sense. She watched him step back, close her tent, and then she couldn't keep her eyes open. Sleep enveloped her.

NEXT MORNING

Leslie was lying in a hammock on a beautiful beach, cocktail drink in hand, the smell of the taco vendor booth down the way wafting by. She was seriously considering getting up from her comfy spot to get a few. John was walking out of the water, drops falling off his strong arms and body. She smiled, knowing that they had all night tonight for her to get to know his arms, and everything else.

He walked up and tossed his snorkel gear next to her, bits of sea water flying up and dotting her skin. He gave her his serious look. "Don't you think it's time you go find me?"

Leslie's eyes shot open, she was in her tent in the Amazon. It was bright outside, too bright. She rushed up and out, the sun was almost straight up in the sky and no one had woken her.

My gods, she thought. Did Alex harm anyone? She dashed to the campfire. The flame was long dead and Dan was snoring, laying in full sun. Alex must have forced everyone asleep, like her. She shook Dan until he opened his eyes.

"Oh." He groaned. "I feel like I have a hangover."

"I've got to go wake everyone." Leslie dashed over to AJ's tent next. She hated the invasion of privacy, but unzipped AJ's tent to look inside. AJ was also asleep. Leslie was less worried now, but shook AJ's feet to get her awake. "Wake up. Get ready and meet me at the campfire."

Leslie ran to each of the other tents and woke everyone.

She didn't feel right though. Her heart was racing and there was a huge flow of tension throughout her body. As she touched the cook pan, a blue spark erupted from her finger.

What had Alex done to her?

AJ approached the fire, running her hands through her short black hair. "Leslie, something happened last night."

Leslie nodded. "You bet it did. That something was Alex. Alex might still be out there and a danger to us. Everyone needs to make a choice on whether they continue or not."

"Danger? Alex?" Miguel said, approaching Leslie.

Dan shook his head. "I don't know what he did, but you know, it's always the one's you don't expect."

Anya walked up.

"Okay. Now that everyone's here—" Leslie started.

"Vait," Anya interrupted and looked back at the tents. "Vat about Benignio?"

Leslie shook her head. "Not only is Alex gone, but so is Benignio."

Dan shrugged. "He was his guide. But Alex was here for research, wasn't he? So what's he done. What's the big deal?"

"Is there gold? Is that vy he obviously drugged us?" Anya asked.

Leslie blew out a long sigh, thinking about how she was going to say this. "Not that long ago, John, AJ, Miguel, and I were in this jungle. We ran into an Inca god, named Viracocha."

She looked around at everyone's faces. Anya looked like she

didn't care, Dan looked curious, and Miguel looked sad, probably reminiscing about losing his brother.

"Viracocha was responsible for the break-down of our ship and the reason why we had to make our way out of the jungle on foot."

Dan nodded. "That article you wrote for Adventure Magazine was amazing. But there was no mention of a god."

Leslie grimaced. "Could you have imagined? Adventure Magazine would have refused to pay me for an article where I talk about a god joining the trip."

Anya shook her head. "Let's move on. I don't care nor believe in your god. But tell us about Alex."

"Well, before leaving last night, Alex told me he was the human son of Viracocha."

Anya rolled her eyes and shook her head. "I'm going to pack up and get ready to leave. If you have something important to tell me, let me know."

"Look Anya. I'm just saying that Alex is dangerous. He may or may not still be at the city, if that's what his goal was. If we go there looking for John, then we might end up facing down a demigod."

AJ nodded, "He's at the city, I'm sure of it. I was sleep walking last night and he woke me when I was at a door of a building in the city. I think it's important, but I don't know why. I'm betting that's where he went and I think we need to get back there, to protect whatever it is he's after."

Anya turned away and tossed the words over her shoulder, "Fine, then ve face him if he's there, but ve look for my John."

Leslie rankled a bit at 'my John,' but Anya was right. The dream came back to Leslie of being on the beach with John. It had felt so real. Maybe a byproduct of the magic.

Leslie shook the thought aside, they had other things to worry about right now. "So, what about the rest of you? Are we moving forward? I know that I need to keep looking for John, but you all don't have to."

Dan huffed a laugh. "Look, I don't know what's really going on, but I'm not missing any of the action." He punctuated that by getting up and stuffing his sleeping bag into his backpack.

AJ nodded. "I have no intention of not going with you, I need to see what's beyond that door. Whatever it is, it's calling me."

Miguel shook his head. "Alex seemed so normal. But, I signed on to help and I still want to find John."

Leslie felt some relief, at least she wasn't losing anyone. "Ok. It's a granola bar on the trail kind of morning. Let's get packed up quick and get out of here." She wanted to find John more than anything, but maybe by finding Alex and what he was after, they might come across John.

As they walked toward their tents, Leslie signaled AJ to follow her. When they were out of earshot of the others, Leslie started. "Last night, Alex came to my tent and he..." She hesitated, thinking again of what would sound possible, but then realized she was talking to someone who would understand. "He seemed to be giving me energy. It was blue and poured into me. I can still feel it. It feels like I have this power inside of me ready to burst out. It's making me feel anxious."

AJ nodded. "That sounds about right, but why? It doesn't make sense."

"I don't know." Leslie shook her head. Nothing really made sense right now. "Hey, also. Last night, did um, well, Alex kiss you?"

AJ's lip curled in distaste. "Yuck. No."

Leslie laughed at her reaction. "Ok."

AJ continued. "What I do find interesting is he was helpful last night. He escorted me back to camp, and then I think he put me to sleep. Leslie, why doesn't he hate me? If he's really

Viracocha's son, does he know his father gave me powers? And why didn't Viracocha give them to his own flesh and blood?"

Leslie felt a shiver run through her spine. "If Viracocha thought that Alex wasn't worthy of his powers, maybe there was a reason for that. Let's hope we don't find out why."

49

DISCOVERY

AJ ran through some yoga poses, focusing on calming her energies, but they swirled. What was Alex up to? She couldn't access any of Viracocha's memories for any reason why he had never given his own powers over to his son.

She was looking off in the distance when movement caught her eye. "Does anyone see that?"

Leslie moved to stand next to her and the rest of the group looked in the same direction.

Leslie shook her head. "Is it a local hiding in the trees?"

AJ shook her head. "It looks like smoke hanging in the air, but it's moving in an organized way."

"Smoke?" Leslie asked.

AJ nodded then glanced to her right and pointed with her lips. "There's another one over there. Both seem to be coming this direction."

Leslie grabbed up her bag. "I don't like the sound of that. Let's get moving. AJ lead the way."

AJ walked in the direction Alex and she had come from last

night until she found the path along the old road. It was obvious that others had walked this way before. There were probably locals out here who still used the old roads built by the Inca and their predecessors.

AJ led them for a half an hour until they passed through the gate wall. It was only hip height, but she recognized the shape of the bricks from her dreams. Stepping past them, she realized she wasn't sure where to go. In her dreams the city was real and vibrant, the walls were up and the road intact. Here she could only see pieces of the once great city. Her brows knitted together, she stopped and put her hands on her hips.

Leslie stopped close by. "What's going on?"

AJ shook her head. "I don't know how to find that door. Everything looks different in the light. From here I would say we go forward, but I'm not sure."

Leslie looked out over the partial walls of stones, some whole walls, and trees and vines. "AJ, can you do what Viracocha did?"

The question got on AJ's nerves, although she wasn't even sure what Leslie meant.

Leslie continued. "Remember when we first arrived at the pyramids? The area came to life as if it were six hundred years ago, we could see the pyramids being formed. Can you do that? Recreate the scene for us? Then you could pin point the part of the city you're looking for."

AJ nodded but wasn't sure how to do that. She thought back to what Viracocha had said that day the pyramids had come to life.

She looked out over the old city and started, "Many peoples built this place. In the end, it belonged to the Inca. Imagine what it would have been like to come to this jungle in the beginning."

The jungle trees continued waving in the wind, the stones

remained as they were, ancient and tired. AJ sighed and thought about Darryl. He would want her to remember who she was and use her own words.

She closed her eyes and imagined what she had seen in her dreams and wrapped her power around the images in her mind. "Here stood the mighty lost city of Viracocha. A shining beacon of civilization deep in the heart of the jungle."

Anya's intake of breath was all AJ needed to hear to know the magic was working. AJ kept building the image in her mind. "A world built by strong hands and determined people."

Leslie touched her arm. "Open your eyes AJ and take us there, before your beautiful illusion disappears."

AJ opened her eyes and looked down on the other woman's human face. "Don't touch me."

Leslie let go and stepped back. "Sorry, AJ. You are AJ, right?"

AJ nodded. She looked at the imaginary picture perfect village that lay around her and made her way to the walkway leading to the building with the all-important and mysterious door. She led the group forward but stopped for a moment and leaned against a tree, suddenly feeling very tired.

"AJ, are you okay?" Leslie asked.

AJ pushed off from the tree and nodded. "Doing that must have taxed my energy." She walked through the open doorway to the next door. In the vision it was still closed, the frame, door, and gold ring in perfect condition.

The illusion faded and she saw that part of the door lay on the floor, blasted off of by something or someone. AJ shook her head. "The door was definitely intact last night. In my dream I tried to get through it, but it was solid and wouldn't open."

Leslie ran her hands along the jagged edge of what was left of the stone door. "Well, we know that Alex was here then."

50

GOING DOWN

Leslie walked through first, she didn't want anyone else to get hurt if Alex was waiting on the other side. She took a moment to adjust to her new surroundings. There was a scent of honeysuckle and it was like someone had turned on an air conditioner. She shivered in the cold air.

Miguel came in behind her. "We should take this slow. Just in case there are any traps left behind by the Inca, or our friend Alex."

She nodded. There were no windows or breaks in the walls to allow in light. She dug in her bag for a flashlight and also pulled out her LED lantern.

The illumination changed everything. It wasn't a building at all. They were inside the entrance to a small cave. The dark grey rock was wide at the entrance and narrowed up ahead. Through the narrow passage she spotted another doorframe.

The floor was solid rock, so Leslie didn't fear that any traps were laid here. She did pause where the cave became shoulder width. She took a second to lean against the stone wall and peek around the corner. Nothing out of the ordinary, just another cave wall.

As she pushed off toward the doorway she thought it was strange that she was so tired— The power from Alex was drained and the tension was gone. But what had happened to it?

AJ, Anya, and Dan were close behind them as they made their way to the other end of the cave.

In the next doorway, she could see stone steps leading down, but her meager light did nothing to illuminate what was beyond.

Miguel reached for the lantern she held. "Let me go first."

Leslie let him take it and followed him; Anya, AJ, and Dan were close behind.

As the lantern light moved, a reflection created a bright flash of light that awed Leslie into stopping. The reflection died and they were back in relative gloom, but Leslie was sure she had just seen something amazing.

Anya ran into her. "Vy did you stop?"

Leslie ignored her question. "Miguel, can you take a step back. Get that reflection back?"

"*Si.*" His voice was breathless. She was sure he had seen it too.

Miguel took two steps back and the lantern light reflected from a shiny piece of metal on the cave wall to their right, then bounced from mirrored piece to mirrored piece. Until they could make out the whole of the space.

Below them, inside the cave, was a city. In the center was an aqua blue lake. Next to the lake was a large stone building with a long series of stairs. Beyond were hundreds of stone buildings, wide streets, and drainage routes that led to the lake.

"Whoa. A city underneath a city. Well, shit." Leslie said.

"Shit?" Dan exclaimed.

"I know this is exciting, and we're concerned about what Alex is up to, but John's not here. He wouldn't go into this place. He'd never find help here. If he had found this place, he would have turned around and kept going somewhere else. The cave maybe good for shelter for a night, but that's it."

"I disagree." Anya had fire in her eyes. "He vould have vanted to explore this and find out more. I think he might be in there, among the buildings."

More than anything Leslie would have liked to walk around the buildings and explore this hidden world, but she could feel it in her bones, John wasn't here. "I never like splitting up a team, but I have to go back out. There are some buildings left of the city up top. I'd rather go up there and search. That to me is a more likely spot where he would have stopped."

"I won't turn around now," AJ responded. "This place has called to me."

Leslie nodded. "I get it." She was feeling a bit abandoned as she stepped toward the exit. "Everyone be careful. Let's all meet at the outer door by sundown, that's only three hours from now."

AJ nodded.

Miguel lowered the lantern and they were plunged into darkness, the few feet of light still felt like darkness. "Yes. You all be careful. I'm going with Leslie."

She felt a little better, at least she wasn't going outside alone. As expected though, Dan followed AJ and Anya. Their tiny points of flashlights moving toward the stairs leading down to the lake.

Leslie mentally wished them luck as she turned toward the exit. But she wished herself luck as well. They had a window that would close soon. If they didn't find John soon, they would have to make their way out of the jungle.

Leslie stepped out into the sunlight and hoped that one of the two groups would have some success.

51

OBSERVATORY IN THE CITY

L eslie stepped out into the street, looking up and down the path. She turned right, going beyond what they had seen so far to see if there were any other intact buildings. In ten feet they went from a tree covered area to a open space, devoid of growth. Instead, it was a field of stone, with a few stone structures still standing.

Leslie felt hope. "Miguel, can you check that building over there?"

He nodded and walked toward the stone ruins.

Leslie walked down a pristine stone pathway. The cave rock underneath the ruins must have prevented anything from growing or someone was maintaining this part of the path. She made her way to a ten-foot high rounded building. Not something that she had ever seen before in Inca architecture. It had a rounded roof of stone.

The door had long ago rotted away. She ascertained that no one had been inside the structure lately. The dust and dirt inside were untouched by boots or feet.

She glanced up at the ceiling. The interlocking pieces of

rock had impressively stayed together all these years. The hole at the top reminded her of buildings in remote locations around the world that she had seen on her trips. Perhaps at one time this building had held wooden steps and a platform that allowed views through the top hole like an observatory.

Leslie inspected the stones on the inside of the structure and then the outside. It was solidly built and there were protrusions from the stones, some probably to hold a door frame, others for decoration. She had a plan in mind that might just fit perfectly with the building.

She continued on, looking through the few other buildings that had remained intact. Nothing. No sign of John. She caught up to Miguel, who was looking down into a crack in the rocks.

"Looks like earthquakes have opened up a hole here to the cavern below."

Leslie knelt down next to him and looked through. Sure enough she could see a pin point of light moving in the dark cave below.

As Miguel stood, a small quake shook the buildings around them. The sound was jarring, stones grinding against each other like someone grinding giant teeth.

Leslie and Miguel looked at each other, Leslie could feel her heart beat faster and see the fear in Miguel's eyes. The buildings around them would quickly right themselves, as the Inca had built the buildings to withstand earth tremors. However, if the rocks at the top of the cave gave way it could send Leslie and Miguel down hundreds of feet to their death, or send rocks hurling onto the explorers in the underground city.

Miguel and Leslie backed away from the opening. When the earthquake stopped they dashed to the entrance to the cave. Leslie had to know that AJ and the rest were okay.

52

DUST AND DIRT

AJ made a beeline toward the large structure in front of the lake. Anya and Dan followed her. She stopped at the lake to glance into the surface. Her flashlight revealed perfectly clear, blue water. She touched the water and drew her hand back quickly. It was ice cold. Leslie might enjoy cold environments but AJ preferred the heat of New Mexico in the summer. The lake was far from inviting.

She turned to the building. The stone steps were wide, hewn from the rock itself. She started up, trying to get a rhythm going but stumbled. The steps were not the same size. She had read that the Inca had created steps like that to protect themselves from enemies. It would slow them down and allow the Inca more time to protect what was important to them.

That more than anything told her that something here had been considered precious. She just hoped that Alex wasn't still in here somewhere. Partly because he obviously had power, but partly because she felt guilty. Guilty for the power given to her. Had he seen his father since his birth? Did he know that she had his father's powers now? Certainly he couldn't. Unless he had a special sense of what lay underneath, like her friend and coach Annie, who had helped her turn the masculine powers of Viracocha into something more her's, something that she could control. But did she really have control?

AJ continued to plod up the stone steps, with Anya trying to keep up. Dan was walking slowly behind them, looking around and scanning the vicinity with his flashlight.

"Ouch!" Anya tripped then let out a string of Russian words.

AJ stopped and panned her flashlight around, something didn't feel right.

She panned the flashlight up and around her.

"What are you looking for up there?" Anya asked as she started walking up the stairs again.

AJ shook her head. "I just feel like something is watching us. Do you feel it?"

Anya shook her head. "You and your friend Leslie are both crazy. There is nothing here but old buildings and dust. No gods and no magic."

AJ felt insulted at Anya's disbelief. Even before her powers, AJ had a connection with her Diné heritage and believed in magic and the power of nature. Here, at the seat of Viracocha's power, and as she came closer to the entrance of the building, she felt a connection. She also felt more energy pumping through her veins. She felt strong again after the lethargy from earlier.

The thought filtered through her mind, let Anya know that magic exists.

As she entered the doorway, she spied holders around the room that would have held torches. The torches were long gone, they had probably decomposed. But she didn't need torches.

AJ threw her hands in the air and brought forth the blue flame that provided light but wasn't going to burn or harm anything. She wanted Anya to see and remember this, so her protective amulet given to her by the twin warriors of legend to mask her magic from the outside world remained cool and unused.

She sent a steady stream of the flame around the inside of the building, dropping a tiny fraction of each flame onto the holders. The flames stayed in place and although they weren't bright, it was enough to make out the inside of the building.

AJ looked at Anya. The woman actually looked bored, as if what she had just done could be done by anyone. She would make Anya regret that.

AJ built a ball of flame in her hands. She fed it her anger and it turned bright yellow. She set it spinning and hot, then threw it at Anya.

In the same instant, her amulet given to her by the Navajo Warrior Twins grew warm against her skin and Darryl Many-goats, her old family friend and medicine man, was standing in front of her. Through his transparent image she could see the fireball and Anya frozen in time.

"Grandfather?" she asked the older Diné.

He was looking around at the interior of the building and nodded. "You called the other day and I was worried about you. I was meditating and asked the spirits if they would let me see how you were doing in the Amazon. Is this a dream?" He turned to look at AJ and nodded again. "No, actually, I don't think this is a dream. I think, you need to remember who you are."

He walked up to her. "Hold your hands in front of your face."

She did as he asked. Her hands were those of a man, big and strong, clean and soft. They were her hands, weren't they?

"Tell me who you are."

"I'm..." She had been worried the voice wouldn't be hers

either, but it was. Navajo and a tiny bit of New York accent wrapped together in her careful way of speaking, "I'm AJ Bluehorse. I'm a ..." She didn't know what to say. What defined her anymore? She was a whiz with computers and programs, but she was also into solving mysteries. She was Diné but was she also part Viracocha? She loved Frederick, her family, and especially mutton and green chile.

Darryl smiled and nodded at her. "You just needed to hear yourself, to think about who you are. You know."

She lifted her hands again, her hands. Feminine, long brown fingers.

Darryl looked around again. "Interesting place. I thank the spirits for bringing me here, but I think it's time for me to go. When you come back, I want one of those..." and he was gone.

She felt home inside her heart and the warmth of Darryl's support.

AJ gasped, the fireball! Could she retrieve it? She reached out her hand and her mind toward the fireball. She could feel the heat, like the bomb she had held back in New Mexico, pushing out, not wanting to be contained. But she put a bubble around the ball of flame, forcing it to fold in on itself. By the time it reached Anya it was a tiny speck that fell onto the floor.

Anya's brow was wrinkled. "How did you do that?"

Dan was watching from the entrance, breathing hard. "Don't explain yourself. Don't tell her anything. And if you're smart you'll stop showing off."

AJ didn't plan on explaining anything, but thank gods Darryl had appeared and stopped the anger that had been Viracocha's. Perhaps now, with this feeling of home inside her, she could control herself.

She felt more peaceful but she also felt tired again. It didn't make sense. She had used her powers plenty of time in New Mexico fighting the witch, but she had never felt like this.

She walked to the closest thing she could find and leaned against it. In the light, she noticed it was a short stone alter, and there were hand prints in the dust.

AJ heard Anya's boots walking across the dusty stone floor as she moved toward one of the ante rooms that surrounded the inner room.

Dan walked up next to AJ. "Look, I don't know what you are, but you shouldn't go showing your stuff to someone who could be a Russian spy."

"Not my smartest moment," AJ conceded. She pointed her flashlight at the atlar. It was circular and words were etched around the outside. They were easy to see because someone had wiped the dust off. A handprint was resting on a ledge that circled the altar. He had leaned here.

Dan was looking closely too. "You think that Alex was here?"

She pointed at the handprint. "Either that or maybe John, if John made it in here. But my money is on Alex."

In the center of the altar was a round hole, as if something had been held there, like an umbrella pole would stand in the middle of a table. AJ tried to read the writing, but it just looked like gibberish. She took out her phone and took photos of the words, made sure it was readable in the photos, then took a few more for good measure.

Anya walked back toward them. AJ thought she saw something in her hand opposite her flashlight. Then the earth shook.

53

DECISION

AJ searched for the waves in the ground and soothed them, straightening out the edges, calming the movements. But she was already tired. She couldn't do this for long and she could feel that more waves were coming.

Dan grabbed her arm and pulled her along. "Let's go ladies. I don't want this to be the resting place of Dan Draper."

A wave got past AJ's powers and rippled throughout the cave. The building walls made clinking sounds as the bricks were pushed out of place then popped back into position. Then a crashing noise from the back of the cave echoed over them. A layer of the top of the cave had given way.

As soon as they made it to the bottom of the uneven steps they ran faster. They ran at top speed up the staircase, through the small columned cave and out the door. Leslie and Miguel were there, waiting.

They all stood outside the hallway, listening to the bricks that shook and settled, then shook and settled again as the waves of tremors came. AJ was glad that she didn't hear any more sounds of the cave crashing in.

She didn't even try to stop the waves now. She wasn't even sure she could. She sat on the ground and watched through the doorway to the small cave, hoping it wouldn't collapse. Then finally the shaking stopped. The entrance was unscathed. She hoped the hidden city remained as well. She would like to return sometime.

"Everyone okay?" Leslie asked.

The group nodded at her.

"Any sign of John?"

AJ shook her head. "I have some clues as to what Alex was after, but we didn't really see any sign of John."

Leslie threw down her canteen. "Damn it. I'm not leaving the Amazon without knowing what happened to John."

Miguel sat down next to AJ. "I know Leslie, but this group is losing steam."

Dan, and Anya joined AJ in sitting on the ground. She knew they were depleted. There was hardly any energy left in any of them. Their best bet now was to get out of the jungle and regroup.

At first, the sound of drums was so low and methodical AJ thought she was hearing her own heartbeat. Then they grew louder and faster, the wind bringing the sound a little closer.

Everyone joined her in looking in the direction of the sound. There was nothing to see but more jungle.

Leslie perked up a bit. "Maybe they might know what happened to John."

Miguel shook his head. "Drums are unusual. Sun and I never got quite this far into the Amazon. I can't say I know what tribe that is or how friendly they'll be."

"Ok. Then I'll go in alone. If everything is okay, you all can follow me in later," Leslie responded.

Standing, Miguel moved toward the drum sound. "You don't know the language. You'll need me to translate."

AJ stood as well. "You might need my help."

Anya mopped her face with a bandana. "I'm not moving. At this point I don't care vat happens to me, I just can't valk another step. Someone come back and get me if you survive."

54

DRUMS

"Thanks for the vote of confidence Anya," Leslie said wryly, then turned and led the way toward the sound. It took them back through the city streets. As they left the flat, old road surfaces behind, they immediately moved into marshy territory.

"We must have hit the limit of the drainage system that the Inca created," she said as she looked around for a dryer path. But everywhere she looked were marshy waters and deep mud.

What had felt like it would be short walk now felt interminable. Leslie had to fight for each step.

But the drums were getting louder. Leslie and the group weren't far from whoever was playing and maybe they could get some rest there, and find help in locating John. That's what kept her moving, one foot after another. Hearing the sucking sound as she pulled each boot out of the mud seemed to make it all that much harder, but she kept moving and took another step, then another.

At least it wasn't raining. But the heat made it feel as if the water from the ground was soaking into their skin.

Up ahead there was a break in the trees. Blue sky, sunlight, and grass announced that they had made it to the edge of a clearing. Beyond the grass was a small lake and a village.

The huts were built up on stilts, almost ten feet off the ground. Unlike the huts in Nauta, these were square, framed by tall bamboo stalks and walls of dark green leaves and steps made of carved logs. Beside each of the steps was a canoe, floating in the deep waters around the village.

The drumming stopped the second Leslie and her group stepped out of the forrest. The drummers, circled up on a wooden platform in the middle of the open lake gawked at the newcomers. Two of the drummers sprinted down the stairs, jumped in a canoe and came rowing toward them at top speed.

55

FOUND

Miguel called out in the local language, something Leslie didn't understand. One of the approaching men nodded and waived with one hand while still paddling with the other. He responded to Miguel's inquiry.

Miguel explained to everyone, "He says that they welcome us. He'll be happy to ferry us to their meeting place and we can all talk."

Leslie let out the breath she was holding.

The canoe was big enough for two of them at a time. Leslie and Miguel climbed in. AJ asked her, "Should we go back for Anya now?"

Leslie shook her head as she sat in the dugout canoe. "Let's wait just a bit. I need a little rest before we head back that way. Besides, she's okay. She has food, water, and shelter."

Leslie admired the village. The homes were in neat rows and carefully protected from the waters during the rainy season. It was a smart design. It got on her nerves to read the old stories from conquistadores who came through these lands and called the people of the Americas savages. These people were hard working and connected to their land and the seasons. It was a beautiful symbiosis.

Their host stopped at the covered stage at the center of the lake and dropped them off. The other drummers watched them as they disembarked, sitting in front of their drums, chewing on something, which Leslie assumed was tobacco.

A host of other villagers had arrived as well. Standing behind the drummers, perhaps a little timid.

"Can you ask them about John?" she asked Miguel.

He nodded, but before he could say anything a young man ran up to Leslie and grasped her hand. Pulling her forward and speaking quickly.

She let him pull her, not wanting to offend anyone. The crowd parted to let them through and watched silently. Miguel translated as he followed behind.

"Apparently, he's seen Dallas reruns when he went to visit his cousin in Nauta. He says that he thinks they have a better farm here then J.R. Ewing. Because, no one here would want to raise a cow. Besides, turtles are much tastier."

The boy pulled her along the walkway that connected the stage to the rest of the homes, until they were in another open space that opened up onto another, larger lake. In and among the reeds, lily pads, and flowers were a host of turtles, some as large as a round table at a bistro.

The boy pointed around the lake, continuing to talk fast.

Miguel stepped up next to Leslie and whistled his appreciation of the farm. "He says that they've been growing turtles since the time of their ancestors. The stories say they once had a blue lake that made their turtles fat and multiply, but now they use the waters of the river to create their own lake. It may not be as big as the Ewing farm, but he thinks it's more impressive."

Leslie had to agree. The lake was not only large enough for

the village meeting space, the homes, and the turtle farm, but she could look out in the distance and see nothing but deep waters. They probably also fished from here.

She wondered if cave with the blue lake had been their ancestors' home at one time and imagined giant turtles swimming in that beautiful water. It must have been magical.

Leslie yawned, gods she needed a cup of coffee. She heard someone slowly walking up the boardwalk from behind them, one boot clomping on the wood, the other foot quiet. She gasped and turned and there he was. His face lit up with a smile.

"You'd rather check out the turtles than come see me?" John asked.

56

LOST

Leslie ran across the boardwalk. Tears in her eyes, she hugged him tight and he returned it.

John spoke into her ear, "I knew you'd find me. I wanted to leave sooner, but I can hardly make it though the jungle with this hole in my foot and my arm. The wound is too open and I didn't want to risk getting it infected."

The boy spoke again and Miguel laughed before he translated. "He says that we could probably take the big man with us when we leave. He's okay at feeding the turtles but he's a terrible fisherman."

John chuckled.

Leslie felt the tension in her shoulders melt to hear that chuckle again.

John responded in the local language and the boy laughed. Then John turned to Leslie and said, "I tried my hand at fishing here, they use a spear. But without my fishing rod, I'm a bit out of my depth."

Miguel and John shook hands, then Miguel went in for a hug.

AJ ran up the walkway. "John!"

Dan wasn't far behind exiting a canoe. "The elusive John Holbrook," he said as he approached. "You might be happy to know that you're wife is here." Dan took out his camera and took a few pictures of the group.

"My wife?" John's eyebrows went up. "That's not possible or probable."

Leslie wished it wasn't. "Anya? She's back at the Inca city. She didn't have the energy to follow us here."

John shook his head. "I was married, but Anya's not the type to come out to a jungle. Besides, she's got asthma that wouldn't allow her to come here. I don't see how it's possible."

Leslie felt a spark of hope.

Leslie and John spoke at the same time.

"You WERE married?"

"Wait, you found the city?"

Miguel turned to the boy and apparently asked for something. The boy took off toward the group of villagers still in the meeting space.

"I asked him to send some men to find Anya. They'll bring her back here."

"You were married?" Leslie asked again.

John nodded. "Yeah. We kept things pretty quiet because it was a mutual decision. We had been separated for about a year, then we were divorced a couple of years ago."

Leslie felt elated, yet exhausted. But she needed to know more. "Can you describe her to me?"

"Picture a stereotypical librarian, glasses and all, but with a Russian accent and red hair. She worked for the Russian secret service as a technician. So, she's definitely smart as a whip."

Leslie described the woman who was traveling with them. John's lip curled a bit.

"That sounds like Anya's sister, Ramona. She worked for the

government as well but as an operative. She and her sister don't get along. She certainly wouldn't care if I was alive or dead, so I don't know why she would be here."

John led them back to the village center.

"We found a pit. I assume that's where you hurt your foot?" Leslie asked.

He nodded. "I didn't even see it, it was so overgrown. I fell in, getting my foot skewered by one of the poles. It took me days to put together a makeshift ladder and climb out. I was laying there, trying to decide what to do next when some of the tribe members found me. They brought me here and have been nursing me back to health."

The canoe of men that had gone to find Anya or Ramona, were returning. The fact that they didn't have her with them told Leslie what she needed to know. The men spoke to Miguel.

"No where to be found," Miguel interrupted for everyone. "I asked them if they checked the cave, but they won't go in there. They're concerned about the wraths of the jungle."

"Wraths?" AJ asked.

Miguel shrugged. "I've heard the story before. Some of the locals believe that there are demons in the jungle that can sap a man's strength."

Leslie waived off the story of the wraths, more than likely it had been Viracocha himself that caused trouble over the years, and the jungle did its own work in sapping strength, just like it was doing to her today.

She sat down and wondered aloud, "If she isn't here for you, is she searching for gold?"

Dan nodded. "See, I knew something about her was fishy."

Miguel sat on the floor, looking concerned. "Or what if something happened to her?"

Leslie shook her head. "It seems awfully coincidental that she begged off the group just before finding John. I think whoever she is, she knows what she's doing. John, can I check your bags?"

He nodded.

Leslie grabbed his backpack and turned it over, letting everything spill onto the wood floor. She spent a moment looking through the pile, wondered about his ability to cook when she spotted a few cans of beans and ham, then focused on the fabric of his bag. It didn't take her long to find it.

She took out a knife and removed the tracking device, making sure not to damage his bag. Leslie held it up. "The Anya imposter had a second tracker. This whole time she's known where John was. She was using the first one because she knew it would get her on the team, and more than likely get her close to the city."

"Leslie, we can't let her loot the city. If that's what she's doing," AJ said.

Leslie nodded. "I know, but we can't do anything until tomorrow. I'm exhausted."

A local walked into the hut and waved at them to follow him.

John got up to follow. "This is Roninkoshi, he's been taking care of me. They probably want to have us join them for dinner."

Leslie nodded, thinking food did sound good. "I need some good sleep and then tomorrow we need to find her and stop her."

WRATHS UNVEILED

A J wondered what the Russian woman was up to. Was she scouring the ancient underground city for gold and would a small earthquake scare her out of her search? AJ considered trying to send a small earthquake toward the cave, to either force more of a collapse or at least scare Anya out, but she wasn't sure if she could control it. She imagined it going wild, cracks opening in the ground, and this village's water draining away into the cave system. She had no idea what the end effect would be and she'd rather keep today's natives alive than yesterday's gold safe.

Miguel's snore echoed through the small hut. It seemed that the hearty turtle stew had been what the team had needed. Everyone was thoroughly asleep. Even Leslie had collapsed into her sleeping bag looking a bit haggard.

AJ had been ignoring the see through amorphous blobs in the air. She had been seeing them all day, but no one else seemed to have seen them. Was it her tired eyes playing tricks on her? But didn't she have more important things to be concerned about?

Besides she couldn't keep her eyes open. Her body wanted to sink into her sleeping bag. She let herself fall back into the comfort of the cushioned layer of palm fronds that the locals had offered her. After days of sleeping directly on the ground, it was heaven. She was glad for the comfort, and her concerns slipped away.

But she couldn't sleep, the thought of something watching and following them had her worried.

AJ sat up and reluctantly got up from her sleeping bag. She walked over to the lantern. She turned it up all the way to see if it changed the look of the strange things she was seeing. It was so bright that it hurt her eyes.

She was surprised that no one in the hut woke up from the light. Especially Leslie who was closest.

"Leslie?" Leslie didn't stir. AJ shook her but got no response. And no one else moved either.

She wondered if the blobs in the air might be malicious. She could see five of them now, floating in various areas of the hut. She reached out and touched one with her power just to see what it would tell her, and unexpectedly it pulled at her power, it wanted more. The blobs all came closer to her, converging a few feet away.

To keep herself from collapsing, she pulled energy from underneath her, from deep in the caves. Perhaps if she gave them too much, they'd burst from the power, like she had almost done once. She sent another wave of energy through the air and it was like plucking a string. The vibration changed the invisible blobs into grey globes of light.

John, Dan, and Miguel were stirring.

Miguel sat up. "What the hell!"

AJ didn't take her eyes off the globes or stop the her process of pulling power. "They're draining everyone's energy."

Miguel replied, "The people in this part of the jungle, they talk about people dying from nothing, from only being drained of one's soul. They blame it on the wraths, something the gods left behind to guard their territory."

"More castoffs." AJ said. How could she slay a mist. She had to make these things materialize into something she could fight.

She took a deep breath and pulled more energy, this time from the jungle and sent it to the mists in a powerful wave. They went from light grey floating blobs to things with more shape, more form.

John and Dan were both sitting, but Leslie was still unconscious. AJ hoped she'd stopped the entities in time. She took another breath, feeling the power of the jungle flowing through her veins, then threw it at the entities in another massive burst.

They lit up like spotlights, almost blinding AJ for a moment. Then she felt them stop consuming. They had all the energies they wanted now.

In the shining light were five men in 1920s garb. One of them, a younger teenager. He went running to one of the older men, his ghostly feet moving easily through Leslie's sleeping form on the floor.

"Benedict?" John asked, and the older man turned toward his voice.

Benedict was holding the hand of the young man. John reached out to touch Benedict and his hand passed through him.

She had turned the wraths into what they had been, the ghosts of men who had been shipwrecked into eternal existence by a god who had left them behind. Viracocha had turned the men's souls into slaves of the jungle. AJ hoped she would never be so cruel.

One of the men gave her a British military salute and disappeared. She couldn't feel his presence anymore. Another disappeared a second later.

Benedict turned toward John, his distant descendant, and nodded. Then he and the young man also disappeared.

"My god!" John exclaimed. "All this time I was searching for Benedict's body, and his soul was trapped here." John leaned forward then noticed that Leslie hadn't been awoken by the ruckus. "Leslie?" He rushed over to her side.

58

PLANS

J ohn was calling her name. Leslie reached her hand out and tried to wave him away, mumbling, "I'm trying to sleep."

"Thank god!" John exclaimed.

She cracked an eye open, sunlight was streaming in. She was surprised to see it was morning. Usually she woke before the sun rose above the trees. "Sorry. I didn't mean to oversleep."

John pulled her up from her sleeping bag into a hug. She was surprised to see AJ, Miguel, Dan, and Roninkoshi watching closely.

"What's going on?"

John moved back. "We've been trying to wake you for hours. We had a wrath problem last night and we were worried you might be in a coma."

AJ handed her a cup of coffee.

"A true friend," Leslie said, taking the cup and a thankful sip.

AJ nodded at the local. "Roninkoshi has been trying some chants to wake you, and John has been shaking you every few minutes. I just made the coffee a few minutes ago. I'm pretty sure it was the smell that brought you around."

Leslie laughed. "Ha. Well, I know I was tired last night. I'm sure you all had nothing to worry about."

The looks that passed between everyone told her that something more was going on.

John shook his head. "We were attacked by the Wraths of Viracocha. Turns out they were a lot of trouble."

"Wraths? Really?" So there really had been something to the legends of an entity roaming the jungle. She sighed and took another sip. Then she remembered, Anya was a problem too. "We've got to get out of here. We've got to corner Anya, or whoever she is. Find out what she's really up to. She could be looting the caves."

Miguel shook his head. "You would think that's what she might be up to. I went and did some searching early this morning. She had attempted to barricade the door, but I was able to get in and found her. She was performing some sort of ritual inside the cave. She had a set of knives and a gun sitting next to her, so I didn't try to interfere and I snuck back."

"Ritual?" AJ and Leslie said at the same time.

"What kind of ritual?" John asked.

"No idea. She's in that ceremonial building. She was on her knees and chanting."

Dan humphed. "Good, let her chant. Maybe she's sulking because she didn't find anything."

Leslie didn't like this unknown. What was it that Anya was up to? What could she be doing that required chanting. Was it something dangerous? "I have to go see. What if she barricaded herself in there because she was scared and she's just doing some yoga mantra while waiting for us to find her again?"

Miguel looked a bit sheepish. "Oh, well, I guess I should

have mentioned that she had on some kind of cloak, which looked like it was an Inca priest robe."

"Oh," Leslie said, standing up and using John's arm to steady herself while still drinking her coffee. "That sounds a little more serious."

"Maybe you should stay here while we check it out?" AJ suggested.

Leslie took a deep breath and stood tall. "No. I can do this. I'm feeling better every moment. And John, if you can make it to the city, I have a surprise to get you back to the ship."

John nodded. "I'm not sure I want more surprises, but I'll bite."

John helped her pack up her things and she grabbed one of her last granola bars from her bag, chomping down as they approached the dock for the village. Roninkoshi yelled out across the water and in moments four canoes came sailing across the lake.

From the canoe, Leslie looked back at the village and saw the boy from the day before, waving, a turtle shell gleaming in his hands.

She waived back, disappointed that she wouldn't have time for another serving of turtle stew. The flavor and texture had almost been like veal, quite a tasty option for so deep in the jungle.

She took her last bite of the granola bar, feeling more energy in her veins, although still a bit tired and drained. But the manic energy that had been there from Alex was long gone. When they had time to just stop and relax, she'd have to ask AJ about the wraths and what had happened the night before. For now though, they had to find out what was up with Anya, and maybe find out who she really was.

59

FINDING RABIN

They walked along the old city's avenue, the sky a deep blue and not a cloud in sight. Leslie imagined it in the old times, a wide flat street with tall buildings on either side. Now, the few trees that grew here were taller than what was left of the buildings, except for the occasional structure, like the old observatory.

Leslie thought she saw movement up ahead and waved everyone to stop. They waited to see if it was Anya approaching, but there was no other movement. Leslie quietly moved forward until she could see it was a native woman lying on the trail, tribal tattoos adorned her face, ones that Leslie had never seen before.

Leslie ran forward, dropping down next to her. "Hey, are you all right?"

The woman looked Leslie over first before replying softly, "Tell me, how do you know Alex?"

This question from a stranger surprised Leslie, but she answered, "He joined our group to save my friend, but he disappeared the other day under questionable circumstances." She paused. "We don't know why he really came out here."

The woman took stock of Leslie's words then finally said, "You must stop him. He's used us all to distract the wraths so he could steal the staff of Viracocha."

"Rabin?" Dan asked.

The woman glanced over at Dan, her eyes narrowed, trying to focus on his face. " Do I know you?"

He shook his head, "No, but I've heard of the legend of Rabin. Alex spoke of you at our campfire, but I heard of you many years ago when I came to work with the Uraho tribe. They spoke of the tribal leader with red and black tattoos on her face, the marks of a great shaman."

Rabin scrunched her face. "Welcome back to the jungle, cousin. I'm glad that the jaguar I sent after you didn't eat you." Rabin coughed, soft and raspy.

Dan's eyes widened and he took a step back. "Me too."

"You've been trying to kill us? Why?" Leslie asked.

Rabin closed her eyes. "I thought you were in league with the evil demi-god."

"No." Leslie shook her head. "We didn't know what he was up to until it was too late." Leslie offered Rabin water but she shook her head.

"The wraths have drained me too far, but I have just enough power to do one thing. You'll need to remove that necklace first." Rabin pointed at Leslie's necklace, her protection from spells. "Please, hurry."

Leslie hesitated.

"Listen," Rabin whispered. "I've lived a long time and I was never able to stop him. At least allow me to do something that might help you."

Leslie removed the necklace.

"Place your hand over my heart."

As she did, Leslie asked her, "Why did Alex want the staff?"

"So he can make his own gods." Then Rabin closed her eyes and Leslie felt a warmth spread up through her hand and arm and into her own heart. Then the woman disappeared.

"Was I hallucinating this whole time or did you all see Rabin disappear?" Leslie asked, staring at the ground and the impression in the mud.

"Maybe she was a Jedi," Miguel answered.

Leslie rolled her eyes. "Very funny and what did I just let her do to me?"

AJ knelt down next to Leslie, concern etched on her face. "How do you feel?"

Leslie did a self-assessment, standing and moving around a bit. "Fine. No different really, maybe a little more of an energy level which in all honesty is normal for me."

Dan was staring at the empty space where the woman had been lying. "I've seen a lot of strange things in the jungle, but this has to be the strangest."

Leslie thought back to her other jungle experiences. They had all been strange, from being knocked out by a ghostly snake to a super-heated god threatening to kill her and her friends. How could she say one was stranger than another? She put her necklace back on. "Personally, I hope she was a Jedi, or at least the jungle equivalent. Seems she gave me what was left of her energy."

John leaned on his cane. "I've stopped wondering about what this jungle holds. There is more magic here than in the whole of the world."

AJ took a drink of water and pointed toward the entrance to the cave. "I feel that we're leveling up in a video game. We just acquired energy from a well-meaning jungle Jedi. Now we go find out what priestess Anya is up to in the cave of secrets."

"I'd like to play that game." Dan said. "Maybe you can make it when we get back to the normal world of normal things."

AJ nodded. "That sounds like a fun project."

Everyone turned quiet as they approached the doorway. Leslie could see that the door that had been lying on the floor the day before was now leaning against a wall.

Miguel whispered, "She had pushed it up against the doorframe. It's heavy but it wasn't impossible to move."

After experiencing gods, demi-gods, and wraths Leslie was glad to hear that it took ordinary strength to move the door.

"Leslie," AJ whispered so they could all hear but it wouldn't carry through the cave. "What about the earthquakes? What if one hits while we're down there?"

Leslie nodded toward the opening. "We all don't have to go down there. I can go and take a look, talk to her. You all can stay here."

Leslie stepped into the entrance and moved toward the temple, stealing herself for what might lay ahead.

60

THE TRUTH

A s Leslie climbed the stairs toward the temple, she heard Anya muttering. When Leslie reached the doorway she could see that Anya was wearing some sort of priestly robe and sitting cross legged on the floor.

Leslie approached slowly, moving toward the side of the room and then, when she was far enough away from the doorway, she asked, "What are you doing?"

Anya turned toward her. "It's about time. I've been in here forever."

"How come you're in here and not out where we were supposed meet?"

"I got tired and I vanted more cover than those valls out there."

Leslie nodded toward Anya's bag, she was sure it looked fuller than before. "Then you don't mind if I check through your bag to make sure there isn't anything in there that doesn't belong?"

Anya threw off the cape and let it land on the ground, exposing the gun in her hand. "I don't think so."

Leslie laughed. "What, no magical powers? Just a gun?"

Anya waved the gun at her. "I thought you understood, there is no magic."

Leslie nodded. "So then what's with the cape and the muttering?"

Anya's eyebrows wrinkled. "I was cold. I found the cape in a hidden alcove in one of the houses down below. And I was talking to myself. Something I do when I'm alone in a big empty cave. Look, I will make a deal with you. You don't look in my bag and I von't shoot you."

A flame shot out from the doorway at Anya. Anya jumped back dropping the gun as she rolled away from the fire.

AJ strode in and Leslie ran for the gun, kicking it out of Anya's reach toward the far wall. Dan and Miguel dashed in behind AJ. Miguel grabbed the gun from the floor and pointed it at Anya. John limped in, using the cane to help him walk.

He looked at the woman they had known as Anya. "Ramona, what the hell are you doing here?"

Leslie smiled, good news all around.

Ramona crossed her arms and glared at John.

Leslie picked up Ramona's bag, the weight of it telling her she'd find more than hiking gear. She opened the flap and turned it upside down. At the top were clothes and other items, then came loud clinks as coins dropped from the bag.

"Vait! Careful!" Ramona reached out to catch the next item before it hit the ground. In her hands was a small gold statue.

Leslie let the rest of the gold, coins, and other items empty out onto the floor. She picked up one of the coins. "I've never heard of Inca using coins." She turned it over in her hands. It was a rough silver coin, stamped with a man on horseback and had writing that didn't look Spanish or Inca.

John walked over and leaned in. "Definitely not Inca. Russian?"

"Pre Russian." Ramona rolled her eyes at them. "The Grand Duchy of Moscow. A group of explorers left Moscow and came here with coins and idols. Not knowing who or what they would find in their explorations. Only five survivors made it back to their ship and only three survived the trip back to Moscow."

"And you know this because?" Leslie asked.

"I was digging through old reports in the University of Moscow and I came upon some ancient papers filed in the wrong place. The papers talked of a ship sent by the Grand Duchy to find trade routes or expand their empire across the vorld. The sailors who returned spoke of a city where they met a king and his people. They said they gave the King the gifts from the Grand Duchy."

Leslie asked, "The men who died in the Amazon, were they killed by the natives?"

Ramona shook her head. "No. From what they described, it was probably malaria. They varned that no one should ever go back."

"You couldn't have known that this was the same city, that you'd find the coins here," John said.

"No other explorers had yet found any coins, yet there is research to support that many ancient civilizations made their vay here. From Norway to Russia. The coins had to be somewhere, so I took a chance that they might be in this hidden city that Anya said you were searching for."

Ramona pointed at the coins. "So you see these things belong to the Russian government. I'm just returning them."

Leslie picked up some coins that looked different from the Russian ones. Silver, but with markings that could be viking and another that looked like Latin. She had seen a drawing of men that looked like they were in kilts on the wall of the cave below the pyramid they had explored the last time she had been in the jungle. How many countries had visited the Inca and never came back? She took one of each of the different coins and tucked them in her own bag for further research.

"Or returning them for your own pocket, Ramona?" John asked.

"Where did you find them?" Miguel asked.

She pointed to the wall behind them. "There's a crack in the vall, it leads to a small cave. There were a few things there."

Leslie started toward the wall to see for herself.

Ramona said, "Ve should get moving, before ve have another earthquake."

"Uh oh," Leslie said under her breath, expecting to see more than just a few things if Ramona didn't want her to look. The crack in the wall of the cave was thin, she had to move in sideways. Her flashlight barely touched the darkness, then brushed across a bright gold statue of Viracocha in his snake form. The snake head was six feet tall.

Then Miguel entered and his flashlight illuminated the back of the cave and the stacks and piles of gold statues, jewelry, and idols.

Leslie shook her head. If word got out about all this gold, this area would be besieged. The turtle farmers would no longer have their land to themselves.

The ground shook a little and Leslie glanced around. There was a sound of the cave shifting and the opening grinding but everything went back into place once it stopped. But it wasn't the walls she was worried about. How much rock was over their heads?

Miguel was already in the opening, sliding out. She dashed out behind him.

"Let's go," Leslie said.

Ramona began scooping up all her things.

"No time," Leslie said and grasped her arm, pulling her

along with he rest of them. She notice Ramona had time to grab a few of the coins and her backpack.

They dashed out of the cave as the tremor grew, knocking them around as they staggered out into the sun. A cloud of dust followed them out the door along with a crashing sound.

61
___

IT ESCAPES

A s they ran out of the cave, AJ carefully added to the wave of the earthquake energy. She could feel her frustrations with Ramona flow into the earth. The tide washed through the ground, sending a rumble up from the depths.

They dashed out into the ancient street, away from the dust and shaking city walls. Then the entrance to the cave collapsed and created a domino effect. AJ could see the dust billow up in the distance as more rock fell into the cave. The cave had buckled. Tons of stone lay on top of whatever was left. She took a deep breath and reached out with calm thoughts, held the waves in her mind and straightened them out.

A bright round light emerged from the former cave entrance and floated toward them. Was she the only one who could see it? She glanced around and saw John was rubbing his shin, leaning on his cane and staring at the dust; Miguel was sitting on the ground, drinking deeply from his water; Ramona was putting her pack together; and Dan was pulling a cigarette out of his bag. Leslie though, she was looking in the direction of the light.

Leslie approached her. "Another wrath maybe?"

"No." She thought about how it had felt to have the wraths around. "It feels different."

"How?"

AJ shook her head then tried to concentrate on the entity as it floated toward them. "It's powerful. The energy it's emitting is intense."

"Good or bad?" Leslie asked

"I can't tell."

It floated toward them, and AJ was ready to throw up a forcefield to protect them if it acted out. It seemed to take stock of them. Then it darted away, disappearing in the distance.

AJ felt her brow wrinkle. She could have softened the earthquake, but had added to it to collapse at least part of the cave. What if she had released something from the old city that was harmful? Maybe it had been locked deep below the ground for a reason?

She turned to Leslie, the others still in their own thoughts. "Maybe Rabin gave you something more than just an energy boost?"

"Why do you say that?"

She nodded toward where the entity had been. "No one else saw that entity but you and me."

Leslie looked at the others in the group. "Oh. Crap."

"If you start coughing fire balls, at least I know someone to get you in touch with."

Leslie laughed. "Well, I don't feel any different, so maybe that was just a fluke."

AJ nodded. On the one hand she hoped her friend wouldn't have to go through anything like she had, on the other hand, she would certainly feel less lonely if she had a friend in the same boat.

John pointed toward the trail. "We should get going. We have a long way to get back to the ship."

"Actually," Leslie said, "AJ and I have a surprise for you."

62

GRAND FLIGHT

Leslie grabbed the harness that had been dropped from the helicopter and handed it to Dan.

Dan took the gear, disbelief on his face. "Are you sure I should go first? What about John?"

"It's better that someone else go first. John will need help when he gets to the ship to unharness. Might as well be you." Leslie shrugged, not sure why he was hesitating.

He nodded but worry creased his face.

"Do you have a fear of heights?" Leslie was looking forward to her turn, but she knew that wouldn't help him to say that.

He sighed. "Not necessarily heights, but hanging from a helicopter by a rope is not something I ever expected to do." He took his camera out of his bag and hung it around his neck. "But I'll get some great shots from the air."

"True, and a hardened journalist like you should be just fine."

He smiled and put on the harness. As per the training AJ and Leslie had done before they had left Puerto Maldonaldo, AJ grabbed the rope dangling from the helicopter and helped

Dan hook it to his harness, checking over to make sure everything was secure. Leslie double checked the rope, making sure the it was looped through and attached at two places.

Dan was connected and the two of them stepped back. Leslie gave the thumbs up to the person looking down from the helicopter.

Dan made a short yell when the helicopter lifted him straight up, but then he seemed to relax, smiling down at the group and giving his own thumbs up as the helicopter moved away.

"I guess I'll have to thank Samantha for saving me the pain of walking so far. This has got to be expensive though, using a helicopter as a shuttle." John smiled.

AJ nodded. "Before we left I had a chance to talk to her and she said I could ask for whatever I wanted. I told her what I was thinking. Leslie and I had to go through some training for the harnesses, but it was quick. I'm just glad we had a good location for the beacon." AJ nodded at the radio beacon that Leslie had taped to the top of the ancient city's observation building.

Within twenty minutes, the helicopter was back. Leslie shook her head as the harness was tossed down from the aircraft. "It would have taken us days to get back through the jungle."

John nodded. "And lots of painful steps."

Leslie helped him into the harness. As AJ helped secure the rope he took Leslie's hand. "Thanks for coming to get me."

She looked into his earnest face.

"You're welcome," AJ said and laughed.

John looked sheepish. "I do mean you too, AJ."

AJ nodded. "I know you probably meant to say more than that to Leslie. You two need to talk."

Leslie checked over the ropes. "I agree." She stepped back, giving the thumbs up.

As John lifted off, he smiled. "See you back at the boat."

Leslie watched as each person in turn was lifted off. The sun was dipping down as the helicopter arrived for the final flight. She quickly harnessed up and gave the thumbs up. The initial movement was a sudden burst up into the air and she understood Dan's reaction earlier. It reminded her of repelling, that first walk over the edge where the rope stretched was always a bit exciting and scary.

As she was lifted higher into the air, she noticed someone standing on a short wall inside what was left of the city. It was Alex. How long had he been there, watching her from a distance? He was holding a gold staff in his hand that reflected the sunlight. He waived at her, then disappeared, much like Sun had once disappeared in front of her eyes. Of course, back then she had thought it was a trick of the light.

Now she knew better. So he had the power to disappear and reappear in other places. That meant it was going to be tricky to catch him. Rabin's words rang in her ears. *"He plans to build his own gods." What did that really mean, she wondered. Could that golden staff actually do that?

The view above the trees distracted her from thoughts of Alex. A flock of bright green macaws were landing in a clump of trees. In another direction she could see monkeys climbing along the tops of the trees. This place was amazing, but she could also do with a change of scenery.

She looked longingly toward the direction of the Andes. She couldn't see them from here, but she knew those beautiful snow covered mountains were out there. Maybe when this was over she'd take a trip there. Mountains and ice were her thing, not sweaty jungles.

And, as far as she knew, she still had an invitation to join John on vacation. Something else to look forward to.

63

BENEDICT'S JOURNAL

As Leslie was lowered to the ship deck, AJ was standing by to help her get out of the harness. They reconnected the empty harness to the rope and both gave a thumbs up. She expected the helicopter to fly away. Instead, a package was lowered down from another rope from inside the helicopter.

"You expecting a delivery?" Leslie asked.

AJ shook her head. "Must be something from Samantha."

They grabbed the box and untied the rope, letting the helicopter know when it was safely disconnected. This time the helicopter did move away, the operator at the door waving goodbye as it whisked away.

The box was pink with 'Samatha Sorrenson and Co.' embossed across the top in bold black letters, then 'Be pretty, Be smart.'

AJ peeled back the box top. Below a layer of foam were ice packs, then under that, Leslie could see a box marked 'Smoke House BBQ' and another marked 'Roadhouse Steaks'. Samantha had shipped them some favorite foods, and Leslie also spied some wine bottles. Tonight they would feast as they made their way back to Nauta.

"Oh. Nauta," she said out loud as she realized they'd soon be back. Then sighed. Being back was going to be tricky.

"Yep," AJ said. "Nauta. It will be interesting to see if we're in trouble. Did they find the person that killed those men at the station or are they going to blame us?"

Leslie nodded. "I'll need to call Devon and see if he was able to smooth things over for us."

The ship rose in the air with the hum of the hover system. Leslie looked over at the bridge windows expecting to see John. Instead, Miguel was at the helm. The ship rose a few more feet and turned up river.

AJ and Leslie grabbed the box and took it with them inside.

DAN JOYFULLY ASKED to take on the task of cooking dinner and Leslie was not disappointed. The steaks were medium with a touch of crisp fat. The red wine was a perfect compliment. Leslie was going to have to get Samantha a great Christmas gift.

John walked over and sat next to her in the observation lounge, pulling the chair close. The view if the sunset behind the trees was breathtaking. Miguel was still at the wheel, getting them into town fast so they could get John's foot looked at.

John handed Leslie a journal. She thought it was undoubtedly one of Benedict's by the look of the age and leather exterior.

John cut a piece of steak, the juices running onto the plate. "The journal was in the pit. It was wrapped in what was probably wax paper that disintegrated when I picked it up. It was Benedict's last journal. Open it to the end."

She carefully opened it, the browned pages inside crinkling but intact. She paged through to the last written page, in large messy scrawl.

"IT IS *my failing and my fault. My men, my son, and I die here in the jungle. If you meet a chieftain, do not talk of gold or rubber or the plight of his people, and maybe this information will save you.*"

THE END OF THE 'U' trailed off, as if he had wanted to write more but couldn't. But he at least had the forethought to wrap it up in the wax paper, preserving it just long enough for John to find it so many years later.

A chieftain, she thought. Could that have been Viracocha? Gold had been what had set him off last year. She thought back to what had happened when their fellow traveler and cook had mentioned gold. "Too bad these words were too late to save Cesario."

John nodded.

She pulled out some other papers that were loose in the book. They appeared to be scratchings from the surface of something.

"Any idea what these are?"

He shook his head.

Then she realized what all of this meant. She reached out and put her hand on his. "Oh my gosh. You found his last resting place."

John nodded putting his other hand on hers. "There were some skulls in that pit, his must have been one of them. At least I know his soul is at rest now."

AJ had told Leslie about seeing the explorer's ghost back in the village of turtle farmers. She wished she had been awake for that.

"Does that mean you're going to stop running into the jungle by yourself?"

"Maybe." He grinned at her. "But you can try to convince me while we're in Hawaii."

"Oh, so we're still on?" she asked, her heart light, her stomach full.

He nodded. "Definitely. I'm sorry that woman pretended to be my wife. It must have made you really mad at me."

She nodded. "I would say so."

"Well, as soon as I'm out of the doctor's office with this thing, I'm ready to go." He pointed at his foot. "How about you?"

She grimaced. "Well, once I have things figured out in town, I have one thing that I want to do before I come join you. I have to go back to the U.S. first."

64

POWERS

Leslie dozed off, the soft bed and the gently movements of the ship lulling her to sleep. As she drifted off she was suddenly aware of everything. From the sound of Dan pouring gin into a glass in the observation lounge, to John sitting in the captain's chair and watching over the dark river, to Miguel snoring in his cabin. Then she could see AJ, playing with a ball of fire in her hands.

Leslie jolted awake. "Crap."

Had that been a dream? She could swear she smelled gin in the air, even though the observation lounge was on the other side of the ship. She had to find out.

She got up and slipped into yoga pants and a T-shirt then made her way out of her room in her bare feet. She paused at Miguel's door. Last she knew he had been at the helm, but she could hear a soft snoring in the room. She passed by AJ's room, not wanting to bother her if she really was playing with fire. Leslie dashed up the stairs to the lounge and there was Dan, a glass of gin in his hand and standing in the exact place she had seen him in her dream.

Dan nodded at her and took a sip of his drink. She went out to the deck and looked up. The lights were off inside the bridge, but she could see the outline of John. He should have been resting.

Leslie wanted to go up and talk to him, but this strange knowledge of everyone on the ship bothered her. She hadn't known that Dan liked gin, although perhaps she had intuited it all and her mind had raced through the details. But, she had also felt as if she had been moving through the ship in that dream. And it had felt so real.

She decided to try an experiment and sat on the deck floor and closed her eyes. Sitting up straight and breathing in deep in a yoga pose, she relaxed her mind. She focused on the observation deck and she found herself moving through the glass windows and to the bar. Dan was still drinking gin, only he had added ice to the glass. It was the perfect cubed ice from the tray in the refrigerator, not the shaved ice that was also kept on hand.

AJ walked into the lounge, grabbed a coke out of the refrigerator then turned to Leslie with a curious expression. "Leslie?" she said, looking right at her.

"She's outside on the deck." Dan answered.

A shock ran through Leslie as she could feel AJ walk through her. It jarred her awake and she opened her eyes.

AJ came to sit next to her.

Leslie took a deep breath. "Crap."

AJ laid a hand on her arm, a move that Leslie knew was not something AJ would ever do in normal circumstances. "Whatever else you can do, I know someone who can help you."

"Your friend in New York?"

AJ shook her head. "Maybe, but I have someone else in mind."

Leslie nodded, comforted that she wasn't in this alone.

65

A SOLEMN WARNING

Leslie disembarked, watching Miguel lead John to a waiting car to take him to a doctor. Her stomach gurgled with hunger.

AJ walked up next to her. "You should have eaten some breakfast."

Leslie shook her head. "I couldn't. Too worried about what kind of situation we'd show up to. For all I know, I'm about to be arrested for the murder of Marlik or for going into the jungle without an official permit, or both."

"Well, I'm here to get the story, either way it goes," Dan said gleefully.

"Gee, thanks," Leslie said dryly, but not really blaming him for sticking around. She would too, if it were her.

"No word from Devan?" AJ asked.

Leslie shook her head, her blood boiling at the thought. "Nope. I talked to his secretary three times. Each time she just said he was busy and he'd get back to me. She couldn't tell me anything about what had been discussed, she wouldn't even tell me if he had actually made the call. What good is it to have a senator as a friend when they won't talk to you?"

They had called for another car to come take them to the eco-resort, but two black Jeeps arrived. A man emerged from the front car, putting on his black hat with gold trim as he walked up. The rest of his police uniform was pristine, his jacket displaying officer epaulets.

"Uh oh," AJ whispered.

He walked directly up to Leslie. "Leslie Kicklighter, I'd like you to come with me." He had a Peruvian accent, and his mustache a standard for a Peruvian policeman.

She nodded and followed him. When AJ and Dan started toward the same car the officer shook his head. "Just Ms. Kicklighter. The other car is here to take you to the resort."

"Are you arresting her?" Dan asked, and Leslie was glad for the question, as she wanted to ask but wasn't sure she wanted to know the answer.

"It depends on what Ms. Kicklighter has to tell us." He opened the door for Leslie.

She turned to AJ and Dan. "It's ok. I knew I'd have to face the music when I got back. You two go on and save me a seat at the bar."

———

———

———

TWO HOURS LATER, Leslie was more interested in a nap than talking to some policeman. If she had realized they were going to take her all the way to Puerto Maldonaldo, she would have fought to stay in Nauta. Now she was truly isolated from her friends.

The officer walked her into the station, past an unmanned front desk. Then he opened a door and nodded for her to enter. Her heart sped up a beat. One table, two chairs facing opposite each other, no windows. This was an interrogation room.

She walked in and sat down.

"Someone will be with you soon." He shut the door behind him as he left.

Leslie blew out a breath that she had been holding. She got up from the chair and walked around the square room. There were no video cameras. She tested the door. It was locked.

She must be in a lot more trouble than she thought. She considered what was in her bag. If it came to it, she could set up her camp stove to heat water and make some coffee. She'd give them fifteen minutes before she got comfortable.

As she was digging in her bag, a man walked in. He was tall and blond, his eyes cold blue. A shiver passed through Leslie.

"Miss Kicklighter, I'm Major Leverence."

She realized the name was familiar. "Leverence?" she said.

He nodded, put his foot up on the other chair and leaned in toward the table. He was wearing a sidearm and he had a bag that he threw onto the table. It landed with a thunk. "Yes. Leverence. There aren't many Leverences in this part of the country. My brother lived not too far from here. Perhaps you knew him?"

Leslie tried to breath normally. She kept her gaze on the major, his eyes reminding her very much of Simon's. Luckily she hadn't been looking in Simon's eyes when she had stabbed him last year, in her fight to stay alive. His body was somewhere in the jungle. She didn't want to know what the major had in the bag.

The door burst open, Dan was standing in the doorway.

"Miss Kicklighter. I'm Dan Draper from the Daily Sun. I understand that the Peruvian government has pardoned you from a misunderstanding. I wanted to be the first to interview you about it and the senator is outside, waiting to see you." Dan walked up to her, ignoring Officer Leverence, and took her arm.

Leslie stood. "I'd be happy to talk with you, Dan."

The officer leaned in toward Leslie as she walked by, she could smell alcohol on his breath. "Ms. Kicklighter, I suggest that you never come back to Peru. Ever."

LESLIE DASHED out the police door behind Dan and they jumped into the back of a car.

"Go!" Dan said.

AJ was at the wheel and focused on the road as she sped them away.

Leslie shook her head. "What just happened?"

AJ glanced in the rear view mirror. "I called Devan as soon as we got to the resort. He was available this time. He told me that he had cleared everything with the Peruvian government, that there was no reason for anyone to come and take you away. That made us all very nervous."

"Yeah." Dan chimed in. "I've worked with the police on a couple of stories and I called my friend in the police force. He told me he had heard that the station in Puerto Maldonaldo had been commandeered by an Officer Leverence for the afternoon. So, we figured that whatever was happening, it was probably here."

Leslie smiled at Dan. "You guys, that was a tense situation in there. That was Simon's brother."

AJ glanced up at the rear view mirror, her eyes wide. Dan shook his head.

"Dan, Simon was a bit of a madman, I had to kill him to escape with my life last year. I don't know if his brother was going to kill me or put me in jail for life, or whatever. You two just saved my life."

AJ pulled up to the Hotel Parque. "Good to know he has a brother. I let Miguel know we'd be in Puerto Maldonaldo. No sense going back to Nauta now."

Leslie nodded but was a little disappointed. She had been looking forward to a bit of nostalgia at the resort, but here they would be that much closer to the airport.

As they climbed the steps to the hotel entrance, Leslie pointed to the veranda, where groups and couples sat drinking. "After I check in, the drinks are on me."

FINDING ALEX

Leslie was enjoying Arizona. At least the coffee was good. She drank the last drop as she watched Alex drive away from his house, his grey Jeep heading out to parts unknown. It hadn't been easy to find out where he lived, it had taken some favors, but she had finally found him.

She stashed the cup then walked up to the front door. Locked. She walked around the house and found a window unlocked.

Leslie climbed in through the window and quietly moved around the apartment. Was she crazy, breaking into his place? Possibly. But she needed to know this man, this half man better. She didn't think she'd find the staff, he certainly wouldn't just leave it out, but it was still possible that she could find it, recover it, and stop whatever his evil plans were.

As Leslie looked over his desk with two computers and four monitors, she wished AJ was here to do her computer wizardry. But she was glad AJ was testing her powers at project X in New Mexico, and Leslie didn't want to wait. She'd get a good look, then leave Arizona for Hawaii to meet up with John. Then she and AJ would meet after to figure out what to do about Alex.

She sat in the desk chair. His desk was clean, far from what hers looked like at home. It was so unassuming for someone who was halfgod and possibly bent on creating his own gods. But for what purpose? Was he evil? Was he good?

She opened the drawers, nothing but pens, pencils, and normal U.S. coins. Disappointed not to find magical things hiding in there, she shut it. Next to the computer were a series of folders. The folders at the top were marked SKINWALKER, WITCH, and GOD.

She picked up the folder marked GOD and opened it. It was filled with a series of letters from someone named Mix. Mix was working with someone named Annie on his powers but they were waning. He was looking for a way to get his powers back and he had his eye on someone that he thought he could steal the powers from. That didn't sound good to Leslie. She took a couple of the letters from the top for reading later, stuffed them in her pocket, and put the folder back where she had found it.

She wandered through his kitchen, then back out to the living room. She stopped at his bookshelf. It was U-shaped and packed with tomes. One section was South American cookbooks, another was South American History. There were several old leather bound books that caught her attention.

"You're welcome to read them if you like."

She jumped and turned, expecting a fight, but he was nonchalantly leaning on the edge of the bookshelf, his arms crossed, a smile in his eyes.

She shook her head. If he was going to harm her, she didn't have many defenses. She might as well continue her search. "How did you know I was here?"

He didn't answer, but approached and reached out toward

her. He took a book off of the shelf behind her and handed it to her. "I suggest this one. It's the most instructive book I've ever read."

She took the book from him and examined the cover. "The Art of War? Never read it."

"Good, I think you'll find it interesting."

He reached out again and grabbed another book, brushing past her hair. Leslie realized she was holding her breath. She forced a casual smile. He handed her a cookbook. "I also think you'll like this."

She took the book. "You left us out there to die."

"Not true." He leaned in closer. "I knew you'd make it out. You're too resourceful not to." He nodded. "I do feel bad that I tried to use AJ and you as a trap for the wraths, but I had that plan from the beginning, long before I met you. I have too much power running through my veins to get in and out without the wraths coming after me. The power attracts them."

"Turns out the wraths were ghosts of men."

"Of course. That sounds like something Viracocha would do."

"Viracocha, your father?"

He shook his head and backed up, his eyes narrowing. She had hit a button.

"No. My father was the human man whose DNA I have in my blood. Just another castoff, like me, like the wraths, like AJ." He sat on his couch, clenching and unclenching his fists, then smiled. "Don't worry. I'm not interested in harming you. In fact, I hope that you'll join my cause." He stood up from the couch and approached again.

"What is your cause?"

He moved closer. "I promise that I will tell you everything, soon. But not today. Any other questions before I go back to my errands?"

"You're leaving?"

"You have two choices, Leslie. I can leave and go on my errands." He walked up to her and took her hand, kissing the palm. An explosion of sensation spread throughout her body. "Or I can stay."

He looked up into her eyes, a curious expression on his face. Then he smiled. "How did that happen? You have Rabin's power. That's a beautiful bonus."

This was not going how she had expected her meeting with Alex to go. She stepped back, took a deep breath, and did her best to push the sensations aside. "If Viracocha was your father, why didn't he give you his powers before he ended his existence?"

The bookshelves around her rattled for a second. Then Alex turned and left the house.

Leslie took another deep breath. She considered putting the books back, but when she turned toward the bookshelf it was empty. "What?"

Everything in the room was gone. She checked her pocket, the letters she had nabbed were still there. She stepped around the bookshelf, all of the rest of his furniture, even the curtains that had been there a second ago were gone.

She sighed. Maybe she should have waited for AJ, because now they were going to have a hell of a time finding him.

VACATION WITH JOHN

Leslie took a sip from her cocktail and set it on the table next to her, letting the swing of the hammock sooth her. Although, she was seriously considering getting up from her comfy spot to go grab some tacos from the vender up the beach.

She sat up and was happily distracted by John walking out of the ocean, water dripping off of his strong body. His gait was slightly uneven due to the injured foot, but it didn't slow him down. He walked up and tossed his snorkel gear next to her, bits of sea water landing on her sun drenched skin.

She smiled up at him, "Now this is my idea of a vacation. Watching you strut your stuff on the beach."

He laughed. "Thanks. Thought I'd grab us some tacos. You can watch me walk away." He leaned in and kissed her, then turned.

She indeed watched him as he walked away. For once, it appeared as if she had made a good choice. She had a man that was honest, hard-working, and sexy as hell. Now, if she could only convince him to stop roaming the Amazon jungle.

PROLOGUE - RELICS OF THE GODS

Bart Potts stood and pointed a finger at Dr. Cassan. "You can't do this! I'll tell the world what a liar and a cheat you are."

Dr. Cassan stood up in return, moving in front of his office door. "You bet I can. I rule this university and you will do what I say. And if you don't, you'll regret your mistake. Now, get out. You can exit through the side door. I don't need people to see that I'm wasting my time with a undergrad."

Bart wanted to go out the main door, but he'd have to tackle the doctor to do it. Instead he backed away. He opened the door the doctor had indicated and walked out, letting it shut behind him before he realized he was in a hallway that sloped downward into the underground tunnels for the university.

He had heard of these tunnels even though he had only been in New York City a few weeks. The students could take them to many of the university buildings, but most choose to walk outside, even in the chilly winter cold.

He shook his head. He was going to give the doctor a piece

of his mind, again. He turned and pushed at the door to Doctor Cassan's office. It was locked, it wouldn't budge.

He pulled out his cell phone, maybe he could get a map of his location, or call his friend Frederick for some help out of here.

"No service? Damn it." He put his phone in his pocket. His small town cell phone carrier wasn't cutting it in New York City.

He walked down the ramp, then looked down the long tunnel of darkness punctuated by occasional dim lights. He walked quickly, the humidity from steam heating pipes making it feel like a sauna.

The hairs on the back of his neck rose as did goose bumps on his arms and he started jogging. He glanced behind him, there was nowhere for anyone to hide, but those pockets of dark between the lights made him feel like someone was there, watching.

He ran faster, his heart pumping and his breath coming fast. Certainly he'd find— yes! A door. He tried the door and smiled when it opened for him. But grimaced when he found it led to another sloped floor, down even farther. He turned to go back but then heard the sound of talking. Someone was here! Probably some students.

"Hello?" he called.

He turned into a winder tunnel. It was full of lit candles.

The man that came out of the shadows had black and red paint across his face and a gold and green headdress.

"What are you made out to be?" Bart asked, stepping back toward the door.

The man blew something into his face and Bart found he couldn't move.

"A god." The man answered as he drug Bart's body into the darkness.

GET A FREE BESTSELLING PREQUEL

I love writing, but I also love connecting with my readers. I often ask for input on future story ideas and some of my fans have even named my new books. I occasionally send newsletters with details on new releases, special offers and other bits of news relating to my Idol Maker series.

And if you sign up to the mailing list I'll send you:

A free copy of the best-selling and award-winning short story, *The Glass Mountain*. Find out how Leslie Kicklighter got her start when she goes on a harrowing climb in Alaska.

You can get the story for free by signing up at www.sonjadewing.com/contact.

ENJOY THIS BOOK? YOU CAN MAKE A BIG DIFFERENCE!

Reviews are the most powerful tool in my arsenal when it comes to getting attention for my books. The more reviews, the better my books do on Amazon's algorithm. I wish I had the financial muscle of a New York publisher, but I can't take out full page ads in the newspaper or put posters on the subway (but wouldn't that be cool if I could!)

But I do have something much more powerful and it's something that those publishers would kill to get their hands on - A committed and loyal bunch of readers.

If you've enjoyed this book I would be very grateful if you could spend five minutes leaving an honest review (it can be as short as you like) on the book's Amazon page or on Goodreads.

Thank you very much.

ABOUT THE AUTHOR

Sonja Dewing is the author of the adventure novels in the Idol Maker series. You can find her online at www.sonjadewing.com and you can connect with her on Facebook at https://www.facebook.com/AuthorSonjaDewing or email her if you fancy a conversation at sonjadewing@gmail.com

ALSO BY SONJA DEWING

Time to do some more reading! Find all of these on Amazon or by going to my website. www.sonjadewing.com

In the Idol Maker Series

Book 1 - *Toy of the Gods*
When an Inca god strands a group of tourists in the Amazon, former adventurer, Leslie Kicklighter, must lead the group of tourists to safety, or face the ultimate consequences. They'll have to get past armed bandits hired to kill them, angry villagers who think they are out for their land, a banana plantation owner with a secret to keep and even drunken monkeys – all while hoping the god doesn't want any more from them.

Book 2 - *Gamble of the Gods*
AJ Bluehorse, a software developer who's inherited powers from an Inca god, never counted on having to solve a murder on the Navajo reservation. If she doesn't find the malevolent

skinwalker soon, she might be the next victim and the old gods will have to find someone else to save the world.

Book 3 - *Castoffs of the Gods*

Book 4 - *Relics of the Gods*
Coming June 2022

Book 5 - *Battle of the Gods*
Coming October 2022

In the 5 Minute Author Series

How to write a novel
Want to write a novel, but don't know how to start? Then it's time to get The 5-Minute Author: How to Write a Novel. The truth is that writing and creativity are within everyone's reach and this book is your plan to get there. This book is full of tips including how to develop characters, how to create conversation, and especially how to get started.
All you need is a chapter a day for your daily inspiration, then write for 10-25 minutes. It's time to write that novel because your story is worth writing.

The Self-Publishing Workbook
Want to self-publish your book, but don't know how to start? Then it's time to get The 5-Minute Author: Self-Publishing Workbook. Save time and money with this workbook.

Short Stories

The Glass Stilettos: A Fractured Fairy Tale

You might think you know the story of Cinderella, but what you don't know is that an evil witch stole her family's memories, rewrote history, and Cinder isn't going to let her get away with it again.

Cinder will explore new parts of the forest, sneak through the witch's house, and even wear magic glass stilettos if it will help her take on the witch and save the prince. But can she take on the strongest witch of the land without a drop of magic to her own name?

Fairy Business: A Fractured Fairy Tale

Cinder, aka Cinderella, finally found happiness but in order to earn a living she's taking on jobs that no one else wants, like checking out the haunted hotel in a nearby village. She'll find a dark fairy, evil creatures, and a stormy oceanside. Will she defeat her fears and face the evil or walk away with empty pockets?

Finding Balance: A Memoir

Follow Sonja's life as she experiences tragedy, then hope and freedom. Ludicrous? A forty-year old woman backpacking through Latin America with very little travel experience and next to no Spanish skills? Probably.

Read it here - first three episodes are free to read on Kindle Vella (no Kindle necessary): https://www.amazon.com/kindle-vella/story/B09JN9LBJX

Find her other stories and books on Amazon here: https://www.amazon.com/Sonja-Dewing/e/B077ZR7TM5